sunshine & soulmates

Sunshine & Soulmates

by

Tracy Broemmer

Contemporary Romance

Published by Tracy Broemmer

Edited by Lexie Broemmer

Cover by Vanilla Lily Designs

ISBN: 978-1-951637-59-0

I used to play competitive softball. I miss it so much, so it's always fun to write about softball & give a character my love of the game. I did play shortstop when I played slow pitch. I pitched and played second base when I played fast pitch.

My parents played ball—my mom was squatting in the backyard, catching my son's pitches when he was in high school and she was in her 70s. ***She*** *was a badass athlete! So this is for my mom.*

Thank you for how you raised me & I will always be proud to be your daughter.

one

. . .

BRISTOL

"Bristol, you know any other girls who'd wanna play that weekend?"

Bristol Miller eyed the brown liquor she poured into the jigger like the pro she had become, set the bourbon aside in exchange for the bottle of watermelon juice, and dumped the jigger of bourbon into a Collins glass before turning her attention to Cole Lockland.

"No." She shook her head as the youngest of the Lockland brothers joined her behind the bar. "Cole, this is rural Kentucky, man. I don't just bump into the girls at my yoga class on Saturdays."

"You do yoga? In Rodey?" Cole tipped his head.

"No." Bristol rolled her eyes. "That's kind of my point."

"We're gonna be short."

"I told you I would play," Summer Lockland called from the host's station by the front door.

Bristol saw Cole roll his eyes. Behind him, Rhett Bailey snorted with laughter.

"You think Taj is going to let you play? In your condition?"

"Mm." Bristol leaned around Cole to look daggers at Rhett and then slipped back into bartender mode with ease. "Fightin' words, Rhett Bailey."

"I'm pregnant. Not disabled."

Bristol nodded her agreement with Summer as she splashed the watermelon juice over the bourbon and stirred the mix. She felt more than one set of eyes on her as she used the bar tongs to pluck a perfect stacked cube of ice from the bucket and dropped it into the glass.

"Pregnant women don't play co-ed softball." Cole shook his head, eyes on his sister. The way he muttered the words, both with frustration and dismissal, told Bristol the two of them had had this conversation more than once.

"Stick me out in right field," Summer argued as she crossed the room to join them at the bar. "Basil?" She looked at Bristol with a frown. "I thought you used mint."

"Did some experimenting," Bristol answered. "It's pretty good with basil."

"You're not playing." Cole straightened from where he'd been leaning on the bar. "Even if I let you, Taj would kill me."

Bristol cleared her throat as she met Summer's eyes.

"Oh boy." She grinned, wagged her eyebrows, and carried the Watermelon Bourbon Blitz down the bar to the waiting customer. The older woman lifted her eyes from her iPad and offered Bristol an appreciative smile.

"If you let me?" Summer's voice was oddly calm.

Bristol arched her eyebrows when the woman laughed softly and picked up the glass. She sipped the refreshing drink and nodded. "Basil?"

"Like it?" Bristol tipped her head, trying to ignore the next Hatfield and McCoy feud brewing behind her.

"I do," the woman answered. "And she should totally play. She'd be fine in right field."

"Right?" Bristol nodded.

"Knox and Branch would be all over my ass, too," Cole told Summer. Bristol bit her lip. The Locklands owned the Skeleton Bar, the distillery—everything here. But Bristol managed the bar and restaurant, and she didn't care for the language in front of her customers.

"Cole." Summer sighed. Bristol breathed easier, knowing Summer would take it down a notch.

"What about your sister?" Cole turned his attention to Bristol again. "Isn't she a hotshot ball player?"

"Yeah." Bristol nodded. "She was All-State this last year. And she signed to play at Butler. She can't play in a co-ed slow-pitch tournament."

"It's recreational."

"Doesn't matter. There's a cash prize." Bristol shrugged. "She's got a scholarship, Cole. She won't gamble with it. Besides, what if she got hurt?"

"What if Summer got hurt?"

"What? Like if I sprain my ankle, it would hurt the baby?" Summer sat down on a barstool.

"Where is Taj tonight?" Cole looked over his shoulder at Rhett, dismissing his sister yet again.

"Jerk," Summer mumbled.

Bristol snorted. This scene or a variation of this scene was so familiar, Bristol knew Cole wanted Taj around to deal with his sister. And Summer was frustrated with her brother.

"He's on a daddy-daughter date with Ellery and Stella."

"I'll call him." Cole nodded as he slipped out from behind the bar.

"Oh, how nice. Are you really going to call my boyfriend and ask if I would be allowed to play in the tournament?" Summer's voice dripped with sarcasm.

"No." Cole paused when he neared her and hit her with a harsh, square stare. "I'm gonna tell him to get you under control, because I'd rather stick a broom with a skirt in right field than chance gettin' you hurt out there."

"Cole Lockland, I'm gonna—"

Bristol tuned the Locklands out as they made their way across the room to the door. She glanced at Rhett—Summer's boyfriend's brother and Bristol's friend. Rhett quirked an eyebrow at her, drawing a laugh.

"I can't imagine what they were like when they were younger," she said quietly. "And Jolene just handles them all with grace."

"I'm sure she opened some whoop-ass on 'em when they deserved it," Rhett mumbled. "My mom's got all that charm and grace, but she knew how to handle me and Taj and Sheridan."

"Did you guys fight a lot?"

"Don't most siblings?"

Bristol wandered down the bar to stand across from Rhett.

"Yeah, I guess so." Bristol leaned her elbows on the bar and rubbed her fingers under her eyes. "Maybe it's just that my mom didn't handle us with southern charm."

Rhett picked his longneck up and drained it.

"Want another?"

"Better not." He sighed and looked around the bar. She would close it down in another twenty minutes, and as he had been doing the past several weeks—maybe months—Rhett would wait around on her and walk out to the parking lot with her. She'd told him once he didn't need to do it; Rodey wasn't dangerous. The most that might happen to her on her walk to her truck was getting spooked by an animal out in the surrounding wooded area.

"Rhett." She backed away, snagged a pint glass, and filled it with ice and water. "You don't have to stay here. I'm fine."

Setting the water glass down on the bar, she eased it closer to him.

"Trying to get rid of me?"

She laughed and rolled her eyes. They'd had this conversation before. Truth was, she loved having Rhett hang around on the evenings she closed. He'd started coming into the Skeleton with his brother, back when Summer and Taj first hooked up. And they still showed up together sometimes, but now Taj and Summer were living together, expecting a baby. And Rhett was still coming in to hang out because they'd become good friends.

And yet, Rhett had a life outside of Rodey. He lived in Kissing Springs, which was a good twenty, thirty-minute drive, depending on how heavy the driver's foot was. He helped his dad out with his horses and stuff around their five acres, and he commuted to Louisville for work. He never looked it, but Bristol thought he had to be tired.

Physically, for sure. But also, just tired of driving to hang out with her all the time. They had fun—even if they could only holler at each other as she worked if she was busy, like Sam, Norm, and Cliffie on *Cheers*. But Bristol didn't think she was all that special, surely Rhett had other friends to spend his time with. Friends who lived in Kissing Springs and weren't tied up three or four nights a week slinging drinks.

"'Course not." She shook her head. "Do you work tomorrow?"

"Nope. I'm on this weekend."

Bristol had been thrilled to learn that Rhett Bailey was a nurse. The night she learned about her friend's occupation, she had imagined people waking up in the recovery room, Rhett's face being the first one they saw after surgery. Friendly and compassionate. She liked to think he would be good with kids who had their tonsils out. It wasn't a stretch to think so; she'd seen him with his nieces. He liked kids.

She had teased him. The night she found out he was a post-anesthesia care nurse, she'd told him women would be lucky to wake up in recovery and see his smokin' hot face. Rhett had laughed at her. Rolled his eyes.

But he'd blushed a bit, too.

Probably that was the moment she decided he was her new best friend. She loved Summer Lockland like a sister already, but Summer spent most of her time with Taj these days.

"Are you gonna be able to play in the Julyfest tournament?"

"Yep. Already put in for the time off."

Bristol locked eyes with Rhett and nodded. She used to play the hell out of shortstop, but it was different with co-ed. She would admit that. It was one thing to field a ground ball or line drive a woman hit right at her, but that ball could come off the bat a hell of a lot harder when a man was swinging. She could do it; she had played short in a few co-ed games. But she'd also seen a teammate take a ground ball off her teeth at third base. Branch Lockland had carried her off the field and someone had rushed her to an emergency dentist. Bristol hadn't known they even had emergency dentistry in rural Kentucky. But that incident had almost changed her mind about playing the infield in co-ed.

Rhett also played shortstop. He was damned good, but Bristol liked to think she was better. She moved quicker than he did, for one thing, being that she was smaller and lighter on her feet. She also liked to tell him she had a more accurate throwing arm. To her delight, Rhett loved to poke right back at her about who was better.

The best part about it was that when Rhett played shortstop, Bristol played left center field. The two of them had scooped each other a few times to make their plays. It was a recreational league, but most of the team the Locklands had thrown together was competitive, Rhett and Bristol included.

"Good."

"I think we should have a home run derby."

"We both know I can't hit anything out of the park."

"Yeah, but you can run the bases faster than me."

"That's very true." She nodded. "Maybe you should be drinking light beer. You know. Stay in shape."

Rhett scoffed at her as he picked his phone up. "Go do your closing thing, boss woman. I'll wait."

two

. . .

RHETT

Rhett waited, hands tucked in his pockets, while Bristol locked the door. When she turned toward him, he tipped his head back to study the sky.

"Looks like rain."

Bristol copied him, walking as she did. The sun had given up the ghost around five, after playing hide and seek in the clouds most of the day. Now, as night crept in, the sky was still gray and overcast.

"We probably need it," she decided.

"You'd say that if I said it looked like it was going to rain for the next two years."

"What do you mean?" She tipped her chin down and snapped her gaze to him. The parking lot was nearly empty. Rhett knew there were some workers still in the distillery, just like he knew Bristol was safe walking from the bar to her truck. He didn't stay late every night because he worried for her safety. He stayed because he liked being around her.

Bristol hadn't figured that out yet. Then again, she had friend-zoned him so damned fast last winter, she'd given him whiplash. Not that she even realized it. Rhett had come to Lockland Distilling with his brother last November. They'd come to get their dad a bottle of bourbon, or so Taj had claimed. When they sat down at the Skeleton Bar, Taj's latest hookup had approached him, and they'd started talking. By that time, Rhett didn't care. Because he'd laid eyes on Bristol Miller, and that was that.

He'd fished around a bit with Taj. Asked what Bristol's story was. If she was dating anyone. If Taj would think it was weird if he asked her out. Taj didn't know anything about Bristol at the time, and his feelings on Rhett asking Bristol out didn't mean a damned thing. Bristol had announced loud and clear, amid all of them bullshitting over bourbon shots one cold January night, that she had zero interest in dating after her last breakup.

She hadn't shared anymore details, though Rhett sensed that sometime since then she'd talked to Summer about it. The breakup. The guy. All Rhett knew for certain was the drive home that night from the distillery to his place in Kissing Springs had been damned cold—partly due to the single digit temperature outdoors and partly due to Bristol's preemptive no to any date anyone might have asked her on.

Still, he liked her. Hell, that first night, he'd been taken in by her dark, wavy hair and dark eyes. The friendly, flirty smile. He knew now that it was part of her bartender personality—that warmth and charm. But he knew her well enough now to know she was fun and friendly away from the bar, too.

He'd been driving to Rodey several times a week since last January with the hope that she would eventually end her dating strike. That he could wear her down and get her to go out with him. Funny thing? He hadn't had the balls to push it.

Instead, they'd settled right into that damned friend zone and gotten comfortable, and now he had no idea how to change things. For all he knew, she could be dating someone else or ready to date someone, and he was too busy ducking his head in the Kentucky bluegrass to notice.

Taj thought he was a wuss. If Summer knew how he felt about Bristol, she would probably sympathize. Then again, she was always nice to him. Always asking if he was seeing someone. Fuck, maybe Taj had told her Rhett was pining away after their bartender. Didn't that just make his skin crawl? The thought of his name being batted around in his older brother's bedroom?

"Where'd you go?" Bristol moved close enough to elbow him in the ribs.

"Hmm?" He gave himself a mental shake. Wouldn't do any good to feel sorry for himself, so as he did every damned night, he swallowed his feelings for Bristol and continued with the friend routine. "You are the most positive person I know."

She snorted. "Damn, Rhett. I really hope that's not true. For your sake."

"Why?" He grinned at her. When they approached her truck, Bristol went directly to the back and dropped the tailgate. Rhett ducked his head into the cab of his truck and grabbed the Snickers bar he'd brought for her. She was a sucker for Snickers candy bars, wavy potato chips, and puppies. So far, the snacks weren't the way to her heart.

If he thought a puppy would do it, he'd be all over the humane society tomorrow.

But not only was Bristol a very upbeat person, she was stubborn as hell.

"I'm not a positive person," she answered simply when he joined her at the back of her truck. She was already sitting, denim clad legs dangling. She swung her booted feet a bit and accepted his gift with a sweet smile. "Thank you."

He gave her a curt nod as he hoisted himself up on the tailgate beside her.

"You see the good in everyone," he mumbled. "In everything."

Bristol glanced at him as she unwrapped the candy bar and took a bite. Rhett looked away when she moaned appreciatively as she chewed.

"Nope. I don't, actually," she argued. "I guess what I am is a good liar. Or a good actress."

"Right." He nodded and slowly dragged his gaze back over the bar in the distance and the woods out behind it until he was looking at her again. "Give me an example."

He stared at her boldly, assuming she wouldn't say anything.

"Okay, how's this? As much as I like the Lockland guys…as much as I like your brother, I think they're all dicks for giving Summer shit about playing ball when she's pregnant."

Rhett was quiet for a moment, taken aback that she'd said anything at all. Even more so that she'd called the Locklands and Taj dicks. Oddly enough, it didn't make Rhett angry. In fact, he respected her for it.

"You don't think she could get hurt?"

"Of course she could." She shrugged and took another bite.

"If you moan again, I'm bringing black licorice for you next time."

She clapped her hand over her mouth to hide her laughter. Or maybe a moan—she wasn't above baiting him. Hell, they'd gone head-to-head over things before: which of them was the better infielder, which of them was smarter—they'd had a state capital contest once on a slow night in March.

Bristol beat him and held that over his head for the next two weeks solid.

"You don't like it when women moan?" she asked him when she swallowed and dropped her hand back to her lap.

"Damn, girl." Rhett shook his head.

"Screamers, then," she mumbled. "I'll keep that in mind when I'm trying to set you up with someone."

"I think I agree with the dicks." He shrugged.

"Then you can be a dick with them," she answered simply. "Being pregnant doesn't mean you're incapable of doing things. Lots of female Olympians have competed while pregnant."

"Yeah, but how many of them played co-ed softball? If she took a line drive off her belly—"

Bristol rolled her eyes and held her hand up to stop him. "Can we give Summer some credit, please? She's not dumb. First off, even if she were playing the infield, I can't imagine her throwing herself in front of a line drive. And because it's possible that she might not move fast enough to get out of the way, she's already said she would play right field."

"Balls take bad hops in the outfield."

"A bad hop isn't going to hurt the baby."

"She could fall running the bases."

"She could fall at work." Bristol shrugged. "I just think that she should be able to make the decision."

"Okay." Rhett nodded. "We'll drop it."

"Also." She took another big bite and pointed her finger at him. "I hate rain. But what can I do about it?"

He shook his head and leaned forward. Hands wrapped around the edge of the tailgate, he glanced at her.

"You can't convince me you're not a positive person. Just give up."

To his surprise, she flashed him a big grin and shrugged. "Fine. It's kind of nice to know I have you so fooled."

"Go home, Miller." He hopped off the truck and offered her a hand.

"Who said chivalry is dead?" She slid her hand in his and jumped off the truck. Before she could move, Rhett put the tailgate up.

"You don't close tomorrow night, do you?"

She rarely closed on Thursdays. Rhett worked most weekends—three twelve-hour shifts and then a four or eight hour on a random weekday. They'd taken to hanging out on Thursdays.

"Nope."

"Let's grab pizza."

"Sure." She nodded as she headed around the side of the truck. "Thanks for the chocolate."

Rhett watched and waited until she'd climbed into the truck and driven out of the parking lot before he pulled his door open. She had told him once he shouldn't be spending all his free time with her. When he argued and said he was doing exactly what he wanted, she had announced she would be his wingman.

No matter where they went or what they did, if they hung out, Bristol was always trying to hook him up with someone. Watching her work a room, talking to women she apparently thought he would be attracted to entertained the hell out of him. She'd never find him someone, not as long as she was off-limits. But he'd let her try forever if it meant more time spent with her.

three

. . .

BRISTOL

Bristol felt the weight of Summer's gaze again. Her friend had been sneaking peeks at her all morning. Summer had been in and out of the bar several times, and it wasn't even noon. She should be over at the distillery, doing some kind of marketing thing or event planning. Instead, she'd been in and out here, like she was worried Bristol was thinking about running away.

"What?" Bristol finally stopped moving and looked at Summer over the bar.

Okay, so Summer was looking at her laptop now, and she appeared engrossed in something. Her normally smooth forehead was creased with a deep frown. When she finally pulled her gaze from the screen, she stared at Bristol absently.

"Hmm?"

Blake Shelton's voice surrounded them, louder now than it would be later when they were open to the public. In the kitchen, the food processor kicked on, and Bristol had the errant thought that it was probably Pierce chopping up more watermelon for her. She hoped so anyway. The watermelon bourbon blitz had become a popular cocktail already this summer, and she needed more juice before they opened.

"I can feel you looking at me." Bristol wandered down the bar and stood even with Summer. "What aren't you saying?"

"Are you okay?"

"Why wouldn't I be okay?" Bristol tipped her head curiously.

"Not an answer," Summer replied, "and you've been awfully quiet this morning."

Bristol arched her brows and shrugged. "I'm fine. Thinking, I guess."

"About?"

She had been thinking. In fact, she'd done a lot of thinking since last night when she left work and went home. The sparring with Rhett had done it. Not the fact that they debated anything; that was what she loved best about him. Well, that and how he always brought her a candy bar. But what they had debated *about*. Summer's pregnancy.

"Do you really want to play in that tournament?"

Summer's name had been on the roster for their recreational league, but when she'd learned she was pregnant, she had decided not to play. She would be the loud, crazy woman in the stands, cheering the team on. Since they were short a player for the JulyFest Tournament, she had decided she could fill in.

"You think I shouldn't?" Summer picked up her water glass and sipped.

"Not an answer."

"I mean." Summer took a deep breath and blew it out in a huff. "I do. I've seen pregnant women do a lot of things. I've seen women five or six months pregnant active in sports."

"Then I think you should do it," Bristol said simply.

"Why?"

Bristol blinked at Summer. "Why do I think you should do it?"

"Why have you been busy thinking about me? And if I should do it?"

Bristol flinched, wishing Summer would miss it. But she knew her friend too well. Summer closed her laptop and stared at Bristol intently.

"Just." She shook her head and turned away from Summer. "Rhett and I were talking about it last night. And I don't know. When I got home, I was just thinking about life choices."

"Life choices," Summer repeated. "What does that mean? Rhett—?"

"No." Bristol glanced down the bar at the cutting board, the knife she'd been using to cut fresh citrus for cocktail garnishes. "I was thinking about me. Just up and moving here. Not knowing you guys at all. And now, I'm managing this place. This really freaking awesome place."

"You want a raise?" Summer quirked an eyebrow.

"No." Bristol chuckled. "No. I was just thinking of what I might be doing if I hadn't moved here."

"What would you be doing?"

"Honestly, I have no idea," she mumbled. "I was living with a guy. Well. I lived in our apartment, and he spent the night with me sometimes. Maybe when he couldn't find anything better."

"He cheated."

Bristol leaned her elbows on the bar and tipped her head back. "He did. But…"

"But what?"

She could say a million things about Trey and not paint the right picture for Summer. And as happy as she was in her new life here in Kentucky, there was a small part of her that still loved him. She didn't want to open this line of discussion, because she didn't want Summer to hate on Trey just to support her.

"He…" She drew in another deep breath and shrugged. "He cheated. After a year, I got tired of it. And I left."

Summer stared at her expectantly, like she was waiting for more of the story.

"That's it."

"That's not it," Summer argued. "You can tell me. I told you Taj and I had sex in my office the night of our first sip party."

"I haven't had sex since I moved here, so I have nothing—"

"I told you when Taj and I broke up," Summer reminded her.

"I was pregnant." Bristol's gruff whisper painted a look of shock on Summer's face. "He never knew."

"What—?"

"Well, he was gone when I did the test. And he was gone… when I miscarried."

"Bristol."

Bristol swallowed hard and shrugged. She shook her head as she stepped back from the bar. "I never told anyone." She knocked on the bar as she turned her back to Summer and returned to the limes, lemons, and oranges.

four

. . .

RHETT

Rhett didn't mind the drive. Even if he'd made it so often lately that his truck could do it on autopilot, he didn't mind it a bit. After all, Bristol—her face, her smile, her laugh—were all on the other end. He didn't need to come here tonight. She wasn't closing the bar; she probably got off at five, and she would have gone home and called him, as she did on the nights she was free.

But he'd spent the morning doing yard work, and after mooching lunch off his mom, he'd spent the afternoon helping his dad clean out the garage. Apparently, Ellery had found two dead mice in the corner yesterday while playing hide and seek with Stella. Two dead mice, three dead mice, hell, three living mice didn't make Rhett flinch. But Ellery had screamed bloody murder, and her screaming had scared Stella, and both of their screaming and crying together had scared the hell out of his mom.

On a normal day, she would've handled the dead mice herself, but since she had Taj's girls, she spent the rest of the day comforting them. And put his dad on garage cleaning duty. It had been a stroll down memory lane, though his parents didn't have near the stuff packed away they used to. Rhett had been amused to find a box of plastic toy soldiers and a box of Barbie dolls that had seen their better days. He couldn't want to tell Sheridan. His mom would kick his butt, but he'd stashed a few of the Barbies in the door of his truck so he could present them to his sister with a flourish and rip on her on a future occasion that called for it.

Rather than sit around and wait for Bristol to call after he was showered, Rhett decided to jump in his truck and head her way. They could still come back to Kissing Springs if she wanted to, or they could grab pizza in Rodey. The place didn't look like much; in fact, the red brick building with the dingy white awnings was no bigger than Rhett's living room. The sign outside simply said P-I-Z- -A, the second Z completely burned out, but they served cheeseburgers and fried fish, too. Weirdest damned combination Rhett had ever seen, but the food was good. Made up for the lack of atmosphere.

Unless that was just being with Bristol.

As he figured, her truck was still in the parking lot at Lockland. He glanced at the clock on the dashboard to see it was just after five. Grabbing his keys and phone, he felt a pang of regret for not bringing her a candy bar. True, he usually did it when she closed, when they hung out a bit afterwards, either on her tailgate or his, just talking about anything from Hinduism to debating the best roller coaster in America.

The lot was pretty packed, but a lot of the cars could be people touring the distillery. The last tour started at four-thirty. The gift shop stayed open until six. He didn't mind waiting at the bar if Bristol was busy, but he hoped she wasn't bogged down and beat from running herself ragged all day.

He strolled casually over the paved lot, eyes on the rolling green out behind the distillery buildings. Summer and her brother Knox were planning a construction project. They'd been meeting with builders, looking to design an outdoor amphitheater, complete with seating for two thousand, a patio, and an outdoor bar. Taj had said they were looking at designs and bids, hoping to lock something in soon.

Rhett could picture it. They had room for it. The distillery had been around for a few generations, but the buildings had all been remodeled or newly built. Only the rickhouses showed their honest age. Rhett loved the tall, rectangular buildings that housed the barrels of bourbon. He liked the old ones like these—the kind that looked a bit like something out of a horror movie, gaunt and stretched thin, the tell-tale Angels' share mold growing all over the sides. And he liked the newer, modern ones that places like Bardstown Bourbon boasted.

The whole bourbon trail was an experience. He'd hit several of the distilleries since he turned twenty-one, and he had grown to appreciate the history and the taste of good bourbon. But there was no question Bristol was the main draw for him now.

He wondered about her ex. The reason she had declared herself single for the foreseeable future. Obviously, something had happened, or the guy wouldn't be her ex. But like he'd said last night. She was always happy; she always responded to things in a positive way. The ex couldn't have done too much damage if she was happy, right?

Summer, walking out as he pulled the door open, greeted him with a distracted smile.

"Hey." He touched her arm as she slipped by him. "You okay?"

"Yeah. Busy today." She grinned. "Gonna go get my things and go home to my man and my girls."

"I heard Ellery found dead mice in the garage yesterday."

Summer barked a hearty laugh. "She did. She was terrified. And that scared Stella. I think if Ellery hadn't been screaming her head off, Stella would have tried to play with the mice."

Rhett shuddered. While he didn't necessarily want his ex-sister-in-law to make his nieces afraid of everything, he also didn't love the idea of them playing with vermin, either. Dead or alive.

"Dad and I cleaned the garage out today. No sign of anymore."

"Maybe they need a cat," Summer suggested.

"Because Butch and Nugget would like that," he agreed. He couldn't imagine adding a cat to his parents' two dogs.

"I need to go see 'em," she decided. "I need some Butch and Nugget love. Bristol's inside."

He thanked her with a nod and headed into the bar. Was it obvious? To Summer? Hell, Taj knew he had a thing for Bristol. But was it obvious to everyone else? Was it obvious to Bristol, and she just wasn't interested? Or was she too deep in the whole friends idea to even consider it?

"Hey." She stood at the hostess stand, a stack of menus in her arms. "You didn't have to drive here."

Watching her put the menus back on the shelf, he gave her a casual shrug. It was true he had nothing better to do, but it didn't seem like a good thing to say. Even to a friend.

"Thought we could get pizza here."

"*Here* here?" She nodded to the bar across the room. "Or Rodey?"

They'd had pizza here. It was good, but Rhett wanted to get her away from work for a while. He wasn't being nice, trying to ease her stress. He wanted her to himself.

"Rodey."

"Sounds good," she agreed. "I think we should go dancing after pizza."

"Dancing," he repeated. As often as they had hung out, they had never gone dancing. Not the two of them alone. They'd gone to the Bourbon Boot Scoot in Kissing Springs a few times with a bigger group, but even then, Rhett hadn't graced the dance floor.

"Hang on." She stepped away from the hostess stand. "Let me take care of one more thing and grab my purse."

"No hurry." He shook his head and tucked his hand in his pockets as he wandered over to the bar. He eyed the bottles lined up in rows on the back bar, appreciating the artistry in both the shape of the bottles and the label designs. Bourbon was one hell of an industry. If he ever got tired of nursing, he could quit and come work in the bourbon capital of the world.

The thought amused him, but he wouldn't get tired of nursing. He liked the work. The patients. His fellow nurses. He liked being around when a patient woke up in the recovery room. There was usually a calm, positive vibe there; people coming through a major surgery, maybe waking up with a tumor or mass removed or something that had caused pain fixed.

Behind him, he heard the door open again. He hadn't seen

Pierce move to the host stand, but he heard his voice welcome someone in.

"Need a table?" Pierce asked.

"No. Thanks. Just a seat at the bar."

Rhett glanced to his left as the newcomer made his way to the bar and slid onto a stool three down from the end. The guy didn't fit the mold around here. Dressed in denim—jeans and a denim jacket over a plain black t-shirt—his eyes surveyed the bar with cool reproach. With cheekbones that could slice like a knife and thick, dark brows over dark mysterious eyes, the guy looked straight out of Hollywood. Maybe a bad guy in the latest blockbuster thriller.

"Okay. Ready?"

Rhett turned when he heard Bristol's voice as she emerged from the kitchen. So did the newcomer.

"What're you doing here?" Bristol whispered as she stopped and stared at the guy. Rhett had heard the phrase *drained of color* in regard to human faces. As in going pale. He wasn't sure he'd ever seen it. Not until now.

"Hi Bristol."

Rhett jerked his gaze back to the new guy when he spoke Bristol's name.

five

. . .

BRISTOL

It took Bristol a moment to speak, to question Trey again. Something was stuck in her throat, and judging from the way she couldn't breathe, she wondered if it was her lungs. Her stomach fluttered with unease as she glanced at Rhett and back at Trey.

"What're you doing here, Trey?" Even when she did manage to speak, her voice came out tight, a little bit sideways. Dead giveaway that finding Trey Kennedy in the bar—in *her* bar, because it was a hell of a lot more her bar than his—was a surprise, maybe not a pleasant one.

"Just checking things out," he answered with a little shrug. The right corner of his mouth tugged up in that little grin, the one that used to make her heart trip a little in her chest.

He wasn't, though. Just checking things out. Yes, Trey was more of a drifter than anything. But he hadn't just shown up here, just wandered into the Skeleton Bar at Lockland Distilling accidentally. Someone had told him where she was.

Bristol cleared her throat and glanced at Rhett again. It had been eighteen months since she'd walked out on Trey. He must have hit rock bottom to come looking for her after all that time.

"I gotta go." She shook her head and waved her hand in Rhett's direction. "We have plans."

For the first time, Trey craned his neck around to look at Rhett. She wondered what he saw when he looked at her friend. Trey had never lifted a hand to her, but on the other hand, Rhett had treated her with more respect in their eight months of friendship than Trey ever had as her boyfriend.

Trey flicked his eyes back to Bristol. The bar lights shined in his black hair, long enough to curl over his ears and the collar of his jacket. That was new. When they were together, he'd kept it close-cropped. He gave her an imperceptible nod and leaned this way and that on his barstool, making a show of looking for a bartender.

"Sure." He shrugged. "Tomorrow, maybe? Drinks? Dinner?"

She bristled at his easy-going suggestion that they get together tomorrow. As if she hadn't moved on in the eighteen months since they broke up. If she didn't put her foot down right now, if she didn't set him straight, Trey would take up permanent residence on that damned barstool until he wore her down. Bristol would like to think she was strong enough to turn him away, to send him marching to some other one-horse or one hundred-horse town—she didn't care. As long as he left her alone.

She wasn't sure she could do it. She wasn't sure she was strong enough to push him away again. Trey had that wounded bad boy thing going on, and he worked it like a professional. Every damned woman to lay eyes on him wanted to fix him, or at the very least, chase away that haunted look in his eyes. At least for a night.

There lay the trouble. For Bristol, anyway. She'd been so young, so naïve when they met, and she'd fallen for that heartache, for that dark soul. And when she took him home with her that first night, Trey had done things to her body she'd never experienced before and made her body sing like never before. And that was that.

She hadn't been with a guy since she left Trey. She hadn't even kissed another guy since she left Trey and Belspring, Indiana in her rearview mirror. What if her skin wasn't as thick as she wanted to believe, and he made a move now?

Would she cave?

"I can't," she said softly and nodded at Rhett, hoping he would go along with her at least until they were out the door. "I'm with Rhett."

She saw a flash of something in Rhett's eyes before she looked back at her ex. Praying he wouldn't throw her under a bus, she continued the lie.

"Rhett Bailey." She sucked in a quick breath and glanced at Rhett. "Rhett, this is my ex, Trey Kennedy."

They sized each other up—Trey with cool eyes, Rhett with a look of hot intensity. Dammit. She was going to have to explain herself to him now. Tell him things she'd rather not talk about with anyone, especially him.

"Rhett." Trey said his name like he was testing it out.

Rhett simply nodded at him. Neither of them seemed inclined to shake hands, but Rhett did move closer to the bar, closer to her.

"Who told you…" She cleared her throat. "Who told you I was here?"

Trey was slow to drag his eyes from Rhett. When he did, when he fixed his hard stare on Bristol, she nearly shivered. How the hell could he make her feel guilty when she'd left him going on two years ago? When he had been the one to cheat? Over and over again?

"Bec."

"Becca?" She gaped at him, stunned that her little sister would have told him where to find her.

"Were you trying to hide from me, Bristol?" He tipped his head and eyed her suspiciously now.

"No. Of course not." She shrugged. "Rhett, gimme a sec?"

"Sure." He nodded without taking his eyes from Trey.

Not sure she had the wherewithal to walk out of the building at the moment, Bristol slipped back into the kitchen, praying no one threw a punch out in the bar. The Locklands had taken her in, but she didn't want to test their generosity by hosting a destructive brawl between her ex and her best friend.

She sucked in a deep breath and grabbed a bottle of water from the refrigerator. With her back to the bar, she heard Pierce when he asked Trey what he'd like to drink. Bruce Springsteen's voice sang about "Glory Days" which almost made her laugh. Nothing glorious about the time she'd spent with Trey. But at least, there were no sounds of a fist fight. No raised voices. She steeled herself to walk out, to walk past Trey and out the door with Rhett. Mostly, she steeled herself for the barrage of questions Rhett would throw her way.

"Hey."

She jumped when he approached her from behind. He'd been behind the bar many times since Taj and Summer got together and Rhett started hanging out around the place. He'd been in the kitchen a few times, too. But the fact that he'd come back now to check on her made the dread in her belly ease a bit.

"You okay?"

Over his shoulder, she saw Trey watching them. Pierce was making a drink for him, probably an Old-Fashioned, but Trey's dark eyes were stuck on her.

"Mmm." She nodded and snapped her gaze back to Rhett's warm eyes. "Please don't hate me?"

Rhett frowned and shook his head. "Course not."

She nodded, flashed him a big smile, and reached for him. She played it casual, like she did it all the time. Inside, her nerves sparked tiny little fires, and she nearly clawed the skin off Rhett's arms. But this had to look natural for Trey to believe it. Hooking her claws in Rhett's arms would not look natural. Trey knew her moves, she reminded herself.

Fingers on his upper arms, she smoothed them up over his shoulders, leaned in on her tiptoes, and pressed her lips to his. Rhett seemed to get the game plan immediately. Rather than shove her away, he cupped his hands around her butt and gave her a gentle tug. She'd meant for the kiss to be a quick peck, just enough to make Trey think she was telling him the truth so he would leave tonight, get back in whatever mode of transportation he was using now, and head anywhere but Kentucky.

But Rhett's firm lips were warm and inviting, and how better to convince Trey than to really play it up? When Bristol parted her lips and flicked her tongue over his, Rhett didn't drop the ball. Rather, he kissed her back. With his tongue. Bristol ignored the jolt of heat that ignited, swallowed the flame, and somehow ended up with her fingers in his hair.

"You ready?" she asked when she pulled away from him.

Eyes locked with hers, Rhett simply nodded.

She owed him. How they hell would she repay him for this?

Trey was talking to Pierce when she led Rhett back out of the kitchen and around the bar. She heard the words *Preakness* and *odds*. Trey was a chameleon. He could change his colors to blend into any conversation, any group. She had always admired it about him, until she had finally realized the ability didn't make him special. It made him rootless and lonely.

"See you around sometime," he said with a glance at them when they walked by his barstool. "Just to catch up."

"Yeah. Sounds good." She nodded and led Rhett out of the bar.

The lot was two thirds full; she figured it was the dinner crowd rolling in. She swept the lot with her gaze, wondering what Trey was driving. When she saw the newer model black Mustang she knew without seeing the plates, it was his.

"You want to change clothes?"

"Nope."

"Okay." Rhett nodded beside her as they walked.

"Can we just go to Kissing Springs?" she mumbled. "Just…I don't want to be here."

"Sure. Let's drop your truck off at home," he suggested.

She shouldn't agree to that, because then Rhett would have to drive her all the way back home. But she didn't have the energy to argue with him at the moment. Not to mention, she wanted his company tonight.

Not his questions.

But his company.

six

• • •

RHETT

Rhett followed Bristol around the curves in the blacktop road to her street. Good thing he knew the road well, because his brain was a good fifteen miles away, in the Skeleton Bar. Kissing Bristol Miller.

He got it. Rhett was educated, street smart, too. That kiss hadn't meant a damned thing. It was a message to Bristol's ex to leave her alone. If that's what it took for the pretty boy from her past to walk away, Rhett would kiss her a hundred more times. He would have been happy to show her ex to the door, even walk him to his car, too.

But that would be bad for business, for the Skeleton Bar. Even if Bristol weren't managing the place, she wouldn't want him to cause a scene.

Still. While he sat in his idling truck, waiting for her to lock up and jump in the cab with him, Rhett was going to think about that kiss. Her touch, her fingers gentle on his upper arms and then sinking a bit in his shoulders. Her breath on his face. The smell of her perfume or lotion—something light and refreshing—still lingered in his brain.

She tasted like peppermint. Rhett knew she hated chewing gum, but she did like peppermint candy. He decided he did, too, but he liked it better on her lips. She tugged the door open and climbed up into the truck without a word. Curious about the backstory, about the pretty boy she had dated, Rhett had questions for her. But he was willing to give her some time to process what had happened. She hadn't looked frightened when the guy spoke to her, but she had definitely been shocked. And most definitely not happy.

Now, as Rhett turned around to head back out on the highway to Kissing Springs, Bristol slumped in her seat, closed her eyes, and sighed. Rhett eyed her with concern, moving his eyes from her to the road and back to her. Had she been in love with that guy? As much as they talked, Rhett realized he didn't know much about her dating history or love life—only that she had announced early on in their friendship that she wasn't interested in dating anyone.

He had been annoyed at the guy, at Trey, but now, Rhett took a deep breath and shoved that feeling aside. Not much he could do with it anyway. His energy and focus would be better spent making sure his friend was okay.

"Lyle Lovett?" he asked to break the silence. Eyes still closed, Bristol's grin lit up the cab of his truck like the halogen bulbs in an operating room.

"Raincheck," she said softly.

"AC/DC?"

"Perfect." She nodded.

Rhett pulled his phone from the holder in his vent and

handed it to her, nudging her when she kept her eyes closed. "I'm driving," he reminded her.

With another sigh, this one softer, she blinked, sat up straight, and took his phone. They'd discussed more obscure artists—Lyle Lovett, as compared to Garth Brooks—one night over beers at the Iron Stag. Bristol had admitted she didn't know much of Lovett's music at all, so for the next week, anytime they were in his truck, Rhett played a Lyle Lovett playlist for her.

She tapped at the screen of his phone and in moments "Highway to Hell" blared around them. Rhett would have liked to talk to her, but maybe the loud, heavy music would drown out the mood, the memories her ex had brought with him. Maybe by the time he parked in front of The Black Olive, Bristol would be ready to talk.

Even if she wanted to talk about farming or forestry or how to make peach cobbler, Rhett was ready. He loved their conversations, and sometimes they did run through every crazy subject he could imagine. Bristol was smart, a good conversationalist. Her laugh turned him on like a torch.

Rhett loved his job, but now he was uneasy about his three twelve-hour shifts over the weekend. He could still see Bristol; if she wanted or needed something, he could drive to Rodey to see her. But his schedule wasn't as flexible, and he had no idea what this Trey guy was capable of.

Two other cars were parked in front of The Black Olive. But being on the square, it was an easy walk for a lot of Kissing Springs. The locally owned pizzeria did a great business every night of the week, so he assumed it would be busy. Not that it mattered. If there were no tables, they could grab seats at the bar and have a beer while they waited. They'd done that a few times, too.

The hostess led them to one of two empty booths when they entered the place. Rhett's stomach growled as he followed Bristol. The smell of garlic reminded him how hungry he was. Their red menus remained unopened on the table; they would order a large pepperoni with mushrooms, a side of garlic bread, and two pints of a locally made lager. In fact, when the waiter came to take their order, Bristol flicked her eyes to the miniature jukebox on the wall as Rhett did the talking.

Once their order was placed, Bristol wiggled around in her seat and pulled a handful of quarters from her pocket. Rhett watched with interest as she pushed two quarters in and punched in numbers for two songs—something by Breaking Benjamin and one by Three Days Grace.

"Not in the country mood today?" he asked when she finally looked at him.

"No." Her voice was firm, but within seconds, she was smiling. Even laughing a bit. "I feel bad."

"About what?"

If she said she felt bad about the kiss, he would have to play it cool. He wasn't mad about it. Hell, he loved it. He'd do it every damned day. But he wasn't sure he wanted her to know how much he liked it. How eager he was to do it again, especially if there was a chance she was still wrapped up in the guy who had showed up at the bar. Rhett hadn't had a relationship for a while; he hadn't had his heart broken in quite a while. And as much as he liked Bristol, as much as he wanted to build something with her, he wasn't sure he was ready to offer up his heart only for destruction.

"Having you drive me here." She rested her elbows on the table and propped her chin in her hand. "Now you have to drive me back home. And then come back."

"I'll live."

"I need to give you gas money." She shook her head. "That's nuts."

It wasn't the best of plans, but on the other hand, Rhett hadn't wanted Bristol driving the highway later, especially if she was truly upset about her ex showing up.

"You could stay at my place," he offered with a shrug.

"I'd have to thumb my way back to Rodey tomorrow," she argued.

"True."

"Lemme buy tonight."

Rhett wanted to suggest that she just sit back and tell him about her ex-boyfriend and why she had needed to lay that smokin' hot kiss on him back at the bar and they could call it even. But she looked tired, a little bit wary, and the last damned thing he wanted to do was upset her more.

He shrugged, not wanting to argue about it. When the check came, he would snatch it and pay it. They could hash it out later.

"Ellery lost a tooth today."

As he figured, the mention of his niece brought an honest smile to Bristol's face. She'd been around both of his nieces on occasion, and the same as every other person alive, she had fallen in love with them immediately.

"Wow." She grinned but jerked her gaze up when their waiter returned with their beers. When he walked away, Bristol took a drink and looked around the place. For a local pizzeria, it had a fun, Italian feel. Maybe the original owners had been Italian, but as far as he knew, the owner now lived right down the street, and he was born in Michigan. Still, the place smelled like heaven, and the pizza was his favorite.

"I lost a tooth on the ball field once," she told him when she looked back at him. "Did I tell you that?"

"Nope."

"I was seven." She relaxed in the booth and put her glass back on the table. "Playing second base. Girl hit a ground ball at me. I bobbled it. Hit me in the face and knocked this tooth out." She tapped at her bottom front tooth. "Thankfully, it was already loose, but it was still pretty traumatic."

"I'm sure it was," he agreed.

"I finished the game with bloodstains on my shirt."

"Of course you did," he answered with a laugh. "I would expect nothing less from a badass like you."

"The girl playing first base got really grossed out about it. She threw up in the dugout."

"Seven-year-olds have dugouts?"

"Have you never been to a little league game?" Bristol tipped her head. "I mean, the games are played at the same fields where others are played."

"But you knew the term for it then?"

"Rhett." She rolled her eyes. "I was a badass. You just said so yourself. Although, my sister is a better ball player than I was."

Her sister. Becca.

Becca who told her ex where to find her. That fact brought to mind a hundred questions all on its own.

"Did you watch the Motley Crue documentary? On HBO?"

Rhett suspected she had asked to keep the conversation steered away from her ex-boyfriend. From any secrets, any painful truths she may not want to share.

As much as he wanted to indulge her, he wanted to know what the guy had done to her. If she might be in danger. If Rhett should be worried about her over the weekend.

"I did." He nodded. "It's interesting to take someone so famous—band or just a singer—and take them all the way back to the beginning. Back to the struggling person that we can all identify with."

"Mm." She nodded, eyes roaming the room again. "Yeah. All the artists out there, I think I just always assume they've always just been that successful. That—"

"Bristol."

"Hmm?" She jerked her gaze back to his and stared at him boldly.

"Do you wanna talk about it?"

"No."

seven

• • •

BRISTOL

Rhett's intense stare made her want to squirm in her seat, but she didn't. She made herself sit still, at least for a moment. But she couldn't stand the fear, the angry bees buzzing in her belly, wondering if he was angry with her. Hell, for all she knew, he had a girlfriend, and he was across the table right now stewing over Bristol kissing him.

"Dammit." She groaned as she tipped her chin to her chest and closed her eyes. "I don't want to talk about it, but I do owe you an apology."

"For what?"

"Kissing you." She sat up straight again and met his eyes. "I'm sorry. I shouldn't have done that."

"It's okay."

"Do you have a girlfriend?" She squeezed her eyes closed. "Do I need to watch my back if that kiss gets out?"

When she heard him chuckle, she opened her eyes to stare at him over the table. He tipped his head and rolled his eyes. "Do you think I'd be at the Skeleton all the time if I had a girlfriend?"

She shrugged. "You could have a girlfriend with odd work hours. Like yours. You could be dating a nurse or a doctor from Norton up there in Louisville."

Rhett shuddered almost playfully, but he kept his mouth shut when their waiter approached with garlic bread.

"There might be some hot women in Louisville. There might be some hot women at Norton Hospital in Louisville. But no, I have not met them."

Bristol laughed softly as she helped herself to a piece of bread.

"Beauty is in the eye of the beholder," she reminded him.

"True," he agreed. "I get along well with all my coworkers. Well." He grinned and shrugged. "Most of the time. And sure, some of them are cute. But no one I want to date."

"Okay. Good." She nodded. "But still. I'm sorry about that."

"Why'd you do it?"

She stared at her slice of bread for a long moment and finally huffed out a sigh before looking at him.

"I need him to leave."

"And he won't? If you just asked him to?"

"Eventually," she mumbled. "If he sat there day after day and didn't break me, sure, he'd move on."

"But?"

Bristol bit her lip and reached for her beer. "I don't think I'm strong enough to wait him out."

"Meaning what?"

"He'd break me," she answered with a dramatic shrug.

"Explain."

She shook her head. "I really don't want to, Rhett."

Seemingly frustrated with her, Rhett squeezed his eyes closed and took a deep breath. Maybe he needed to calm himself. Bristol watched him closely as he opened his eyes and finally reached for his own piece of garlic bread.

"Did he hurt you?"

He had hurt her, yes, but not in the way Rhett meant. Still, she couldn't find her voice to answer him.

"Bristol?"

She licked her lips when Rhett dropped his bread on his plate and reached over the table to cover her hand.

"Did he hurt you?"

"No." She shook her head. "Not like that."

"Are you sure?" He squeezed her hand gently before drawing away.

"Did you look at him, Rhett? Of course he hurt me. I walked out on him, because I couldn't deal with it anymore." She swallowed a drink of beer. "He's not going to threaten me. He won't lift a finger to me. But if he doesn't leave, he's gonna drag me right back in."

"What do you mean?"

"How can a woman look at him and not want to love him?"

Rhett's answering frown was severe.

"So, because he's good-looking? You'll fall for him again?"

"Because he's a walking heartache. He's like a big heap of dark eyes and pain and arrogance."

"And that turns you on?" Rhett rolled his eyes. "Why do women fall for that?"

Bristol nibbled on her bread. Trey had mommy issues, but she didn't want to discuss that with Rhett. Her friend wouldn't have any sympathy for him, that was obvious. And Bristol had always had too much, equally obvious.

"He's actually a good guy," she said softly. "Kind. Generous."

"But?"

"He just forgets to come home most nights."

"Meaning, he can't keep it in his pants."

Bristol nodded. "Yeah. That, too."

They settled into silence for a while, both picking at their bread. Neither of them was talking when their pizza was delivered. Bristol reached for the plastic server and wedged it under a giant triangular slice. She plated it, handed it over to him, and selected another for herself.

"How long has it been?" Rhett took a drink. "Since you left him?"

"Eighteen months," she mumbled. "Give or take."

"What drove you to it? To leaving?"

"Seriously?" She drew back like Rhett had threatened to punch her. "We lived together for a year. He probably spent a third of those nights with someone else."

"Big fight?"

"No." She shook her head. "In fact, I tried to slip away without him noticing. He was gone when I came down to

Rodey to interview. Had no idea I'd even been out of town that weekend." She avoided Rhett's eyes, memories of the pregnancy test and the miscarriage making her eyes water. "He missed things. Things he shouldn't have missed. If I had stayed in Belspring, he would have talked me right back into his bed."

"Well, I hope you got something out of it."

Still avoiding his eyes, she nodded. "I was twenty-two when he came into the restaurant where I worked. He charmed me. I think I was in love with him before that first night ended."

"And you really think he could charm his way back into your heart now?"

Probably not. Not after the whole deal with the baby. But she wasn't sure. Trey was a good guy, when he wasn't cruising for something new to take away that lingering heartbreak he had. Something to fill the hole inside him. He was fun; they used to laugh together.

And she'd been alone for the year and a half since she left him. True, that was by her choice, but still. She sometimes wished for someone to wake up with in the mornings. And more than once, she had wished for it to be Trey.

"I don't know," she admitted. "It's just…there's a lot of water under that bridge. And I don't want to go near it, Rhett. I don't wanna drag all that back up."

"He's never called you?"

"Hmm?" Intent on picking her slice of pizza up without making a mess, Bristol concentrated on the food rather than look at Rhett.

"You left him over a year ago, and he never called you. But he showed up now out of the blue."

"Why are you making such a big deal about this?" she whispered, finally meeting his eyes.

"Because you're my friend, and it bothers me that I don't know this about you. And that he's bothering you."

"You've never told me your dating history."

"Ask away." He shrugged. "I'm an open book."

"He didn't call because I got a new phone."

"So, you were trying to hide from him?" He polished off his first piece with a giant-sized last bite and reached for another slice.

"I mean, I didn't change my name or steal someone else's social security number." She sighed. "I didn't even color my hair. I just got a new phone so he couldn't call me."

"So, something big happened. At some point."

"I swear to you he never physically hurt me."

"There are other kinds of abuse, Bristol." Rhett pointed a finger at her. "Just know, if he sticks around and bothers you, I'll be on his ass."

Bristol chewed silently for a moment and finally nodded.

"I'm sure he'll leave. After…" She cleared her throat. "After he saw me kiss you. He might have cheated, but he didn't hit on women in relationships."

"Okay." Rhett nodded. "Well, if you need a fake boyfriend again when he's around, you give me a holler. But if he hurts you, I will kick his ass."

Bristol chuckled softly, but she nodded. "Thanks, Rhett."

"That's what friends are for, right?"

eight

. . .

BRISTOL

Summer's text had surprised her, but Bristol decided she was happy to be driving to Kissing Springs Saturday morning. When she had told Summer she didn't have to work, her friend had asked her to meet her at French Kiss Coffee. Bristol had been awake since six, but she hadn't dragged herself out of bed until almost seven-thirty. She had never been one to sleep in, even on weekends, but she didn't always pop out of bed with a smile on her face, either.

She'd been tossing and turning, worrying about Trey showing up. And finally, after going through the whole damned thing—the night she and Trey met, taking him home with her, falling for him, living with him, leaving him, and the scenario Thursday night when she had panicked and announced she was dating Rhett—she'd made herself get up. Wallowing in memories, good or bad, wasn't going to make her feel better. And worrying about what Trey was up to wouldn't change a damned thing. Trey would do what he wanted, whether that be to pick away at her armor for a few days and see if he could break her down or moving on to

Bardstown or Kissing Springs or Nashville or some other southern location. He'd hang around the area for a while, no doubt.

Bristol just hoped to hell he didn't stick too close to Rodey.

When her phone had beeped earlier, when Summer texted, she'd assumed it was Trey. After all, if Becca told him Bristol was living in Rodey, Kentucky, then what would have stopped her from giving him Bristol's new number? Showered, dressed, and swiping on a bit of mascara, Bristol took her time looking at the message.

She'd been telling herself since Thursday night that she was fine, she was strong, she had changed. Trey could root around here for a bit and sweet talk her all he wanted, but she was immune to his charm. But the way her whole body sagged in relief when she saw the text was from Summer told a different story.

She listened to country music as she drove; something she had only started doing when she moved to Kentucky. Before, when she lived in Indiana, she'd been more into classic rock. The country sounds made her think about Rhett. They had a good time the other night, after the disaster with Trey showing up and Bristol losing her shit and kissing Rhett. He had been good-natured about it, but Bristol still felt guilty for using him that way.

He had worked a twelve-hour shift yesterday, and Bristol had worked eight. She'd come home after she left the Skeleton Bar, washed her truck, and made herself dinner. Sometimes nuking leftovers in the microwave took all her energy and brain power, but last night, she sliced peppers and mushrooms and tossed them in spaghetti sauce, boiled some noodles, and chopped up a salad. Wasn't gourmet. Wasn't even totally homemade, but it kept her busy, and dinner was good.

She watched a movie while she ate, listened to a true crime podcast while she cleaned her kitchen, and crashed on the couch with a book later. When Rhett texted her after he got home, she called him, and they hung on the phone while he fixed dinner, which amounted to reheating something his mom had made and dropped by for him.

Summers in Kissing Springs were fun, though Bristol kind of liked last winter even better. The first year she had moved to the area, she had come to Kissing Springs several times—she'd brought her parents and sister to dinner at Two Fourteen, she'd gone to the diner a few times, and she shopped the boutiques now and then. But then last winter, she'd discovered the Male-Revue—a bunch of single dads working as stripping Santas. Bristol had invited a girlfriend from college to come down, and they'd had fun, first at the Boyd Theater watching the show, and then they'd gone to the Bourbon Boot Scoot for drinks and dancing.

Parking spaces were often hard to come by, and today was no exception. Bristol made her way around the complete square once before spotting a beat-up Ford Fiesta backing out. Foot on the brake, signal on, she shifted her gaze to the square itself for a moment. Dappled sunlight fell through the trees and kissed the grass, thick and green like carpet. If she wished anything were different about where she lived right now, it would be this. Rodey, the tiny little town where she lived, boasted a population of 77. Maybe 79. Many of which were Locklands. There was a main road into Rodey, two crossroads, and a whole network of gravel offshoots. The pizza joint sat on the main road down the block from an ugly little thrift shop. The Iron Stag was tucked away, deceptively ordinary-looking, on one of those gravel off-shoots. And there was a fresh market on one of the crossroads. Bristol didn't know how fresh it really was, considering she shopped there and saw what she would swear to be the same painted letters in the front window every time.

Sale. Today only.

At least the bread and the dairy products were fresh, she decided, as she glanced at the parking space and eased off the brake. She pulled her truck in between a motorcycle and an SUV, thankful she hadn't seen that shiny new Mustang on her drive.

With any luck, Trey had already grown tired of the Bible Belt and headed back the other way.

Bristol laughed at herself as she slid down from the driver's seat and planted her sandals on the asphalt. She didn't have much luck at all—good or bad, really—but, odds were she wouldn't get rid of him so easily.

Slipping her purse strap over her shoulder, she hurried to the corner, looked to make sure there was no traffic, and crossed the street. She didn't lock her truck, nothing in it at the moment to worry about. She passed several groups of people, most of them probably tourists, as she made her way to French Kiss. As much as she needed the coffee—a relentless headache had dug into her brain just as she was ready to leave her place—she found herself smiling as she walked.

The Trey situation aside, and the kissing her best friend thing aside, too—hard to push her embarrassment about that away, but she was trying—she loved being here. When she had packed up and left Trey, left Indiana, she'd had a niggling sense of doubt. Running away wasn't the answer. And yet, now that she was here, she felt less like she had run away and more that she had run toward her future. Her life here was good. She loved her job. She loved the Lockland family. And she had made friends. In time, maybe she would be ready for love. Marriage. Whatever that life might look like for her.

Today, she would be happy the sun was out. Thrilled to be dressed in cut-off denim shorts and a yellow t-shirt with an off-white daisy on it. Happy to wiggle her toes in her open-toed sandals. She reveled in the feel of the breeze in her hair. This, she reminded herself, is why she had left him. And exactly why she couldn't go back to him. Trey Kennedy's bad boy persona, his dark, brooding side, had swallowed her whole, and she had forgotten everything else existed when she was with him.

That wasn't love.

She'd never had it, not really. She dated a boy in high school for two years, and they had been glued at the hip. They'd been each other's firsts, and they had said those three words. But looking back on that time now, Bristol knew even then they wouldn't last. They wanted different things in life. Andrew wanted to play football for Georgia. Bristol wanted to focus on her academic career. Andrew wanted to graduate, get married at twenty-five—not twenty-four or twenty-six. He wanted babies when he was twenty-seven and twenty-nine, boys—as if he thought you could put a custom order in—and he wanted to coach high school, if not college, football.

They'd had fun. And Andrew had been good to her, better than Trey if cheating mattered, but Bristol had no interest in a severe timeline for her life. She wanted to study. She graduated with honors. Studied business. Hung out with her suite mates. And made great tips as a waitress.

While she wanted to get married, she didn't care if that happened at twenty-two or thirty-two. When she was younger, she wanted kids, but she didn't have a set number or a definite time period scheduled for that. She didn't care if she had boys or girls or ended up with a puppy instead. And the last damned thing she wanted was to tie herself to the college football drama Andrew and his dad were obsessed with.

So, even though Andrew had told her he loved her, even though she'd said it back, she'd known even then, it was just high school love. And even though Trey had told her he loved her, and she'd said it back and meant it, Trey only loved her when she was in his sight. Out of sight, out of mind. He roamed the bars and clubs, always on the lookout for someone to play around with, claiming it didn't mean anything.

"Hey!" Summer appeared before her, three steps from the door of French Kiss. "Want to sit outside?"

"Absolutely, yes," Bristol answered with a firm nod.

"How are you?" Summer grabbed her for a quick hug. "You looked kind of lost in thought."

Bristol snorted softly. "You could say that."

"Let's order and come back out."

Bristol nodded and followed her friend into the coffee shop.

nine

. . .

BRISTOL

Disappointed Gary wasn't taking orders today, Bristol ordered an iced latte and moved aside so Summer could order. Gary, the owner of French Kiss, was fun—his animated conversations always brought a smile to everyone in the place. She settled for watching Summer, amused by her friend's indecision, and even more amused by Summer's final selection of a strawberry banana smoothie.

"I don't want the caffeine," Summer said with a self-deprecating laugh. "I mean, I want it. But I'm trying to cut back."

"I get it," Bristol answered with a nod. "Where were you yesterday? I didn't see you at work all day."

"I had a checkup."

Bristol flinched. "Everything okay?"

"Yeah. Just a checkup."

"Good."

"Taj might make me nuts before I have this baby," Summer mumbled. Before Bristol could laugh, Summer cringed and shook her head. "I'm sorry. I shouldn't say that."

"What—"

"Bristle?"

Bristol blinked, unprepared for the barista to butcher her name.

"Wow. Guess that's me." She rolled her eyes as she stepped around Summer to get her drink. She thanked the barista, looked at her plastic cup to see that the kid who had taken her order had indeed spelled it *Bristle*, and shook her head. She peeled the wrapper back from a straw, tossed it in the garbage can, and stuck the straw in her drink. Popping it in her mouth, she took a long pull as she moseyed back over to stand by Summer.

"What are you sorry for?" she asked.

"Griping about Taj making me nuts." Summer looked up from her phone. "I mean, at least I have Taj. He's very involved."

Realizing what Summer was getting at, Bristol sucked in a deep breath this time and let it out in a frustrated huff.

"Summer, don't do that." She laid her hand on her friend's arm and shook her head when Summer started to argue. "Please, don't. I didn't tell you that to make you second guess everything you say to me."

"Maybe not, but—"

Summer sighed, obviously flustered when her name was called. She made big eyes at Bristol and slipped away to get her smoothie. Bristol wished now that she hadn't told Summer about Trey. About getting pregnant and losing the baby—that he'd never even known. She certainly hadn't meant to make Summer feel guilty.

Bristol turned and led Summer back outside when her friend had her smoothie and a straw in hand. There were a few two-top tables on the sidewalk, and Bristol thought there was a small courtyard behind the place. But this worked. She liked the view of the square and the tourist hustle and bustle out here in front.

She grabbed a chair at one of the open tables and looked over her shoulder at Summer.

"This okay?"

"Perfect." Summer leaned over to set her cup on the table and pulled a second chair out to sit. "Listen, I know you didn't tell me about—you didn't tell me to make me feel bad. I get that. But as your friend, it makes me sad for you. That's all. And there will probably be a hundred times in the next several months that I complain about something to do with this baby. But I don't mean it. I'm so excited."

"I know you are." Bristol sat back in her chair with a big smile. "And you should be. What you have with Taj is very different from me and Trey."

"But think about it." Summer sounded dreamy. She stared at something over Bristol's shoulder. "If you'd had the baby, our kids could have been friends."

Bristol sat for a moment, unsure how to respond. She hadn't been pregnant long enough to work out how she felt about it.

"If I'd had the baby, I would never have left Belspring. Maybe I would still be playing house with Trey. Looking the other way."

"Bristol—"

"Actually, it wasn't even like I was looking the other way. I knew he was cheating. He knew I knew. And he would come back eventually and say he was sorry. Sometimes he really groveled. Blamed it on his mommy issues and said being with the other women just filled a physical ache. That I was the woman he loved."

"I can't imagine you being in a relationship like that."

Bristol took a sip of her coffee and arched her eyebrows. "Well, good. Maybe that means I've grown a bit since I've been here. I loved him. I loved him so much, Summer. And I think he did love me, but I couldn't save him. For a while, I really thought I would be the one to make him happy. But I couldn't love him enough to make him happy. I don't think anyone ever could."

Summer nodded.

"Did you want the baby?"

Bristol rolled her lips inward and breathed deeply through her nose. She finally met Summer's eyes and shrugged.

"I don't know. I would have kept it if things had gone well. And I want kids, sure. But was I ready for a baby then? No. I wasn't. He sure wasn't."

"I just wish you could have talked to someone about it."

Bristol shook her head and eyed an older couple as they walked into French Kiss.

"I couldn't tell my sister. She was too young. And I just…I couldn't bring myself to talk about it to my mom. It was over so fast. Figured it was best just to forget it."

From the corner of her eye, she saw Summer nod again. Satisfied that the subject was put to rest again, Bristol looked back at her friend.

“Well, maybe someday you’ll find someone and have another chance,” Summer offered. “And then our kids can grow up together.”

The possibility made Bristol smile.

“I have to find someone first.”

“Well…speaking of which…” Summer cleared her throat.

“Speaking of which, what?” Bristol tipped her head with a frown. She squirmed in her seat, sensing suddenly that Summer had invited her for coffee for a reason.

“I heard from a little birdie you and Rhett shared a pretty steamy kiss the other night.”

ten

. . .

RHETT

Satisfied that his elderly patient's respiration was good, Rhett tapped the computer screen and flashed his ID badge at the camera. When the program opened to Mr. Harvey's file, Rhett recorded the man's vitals and the time for administering pain medication. Martin Harvey had been in recovery in Rhett's care before when he'd had his left knee replaced two years ago. The old man had made a big impression on him with his upbeat demeanor. Any time Rhett had checked in on him to take his vitals or check his pain levels, Mr. Harvey had insisted he was good.

I woke up today.

Mr. Harvey's favorite line. Rhett liked it well enough he still remembered it, and he tried to remind himself of the simple bit of gratitude on tough days. Not that he had that many tough days; those he did have were usually more job-related than personal. Rhett had cared for a few patients in his years as a PACU nurse who didn't recover from their procedures—whether from issues with the anesthesia or because of underlying conditions, such as the medical reasons that had dictated surgery to begin with.

Taj had called him last night.

Rhett had blown him off.

Now, as he left Mr. Harvey's bedside, he felt a little stab of guilt. Most likely, Taj hadn't needed anything. He had probably just called to bullshit with Rhett; they did that now and then. More so now that Taj was happily settled in with Summer. But on the other hand, Taj had spent some rough times on his own, after he split with Marley.

When Taj called last night, Rhett had barely cleared his doorway, coming home from work. He was beat. He wanted a shower. And something to eat. He'd made a pitstop in his kitchen, downed a glass of water, and stripped down, trailing clothes through his bedroom on the way to the bathroom for a shower. The hot water had felt good enough to linger for a bit, the shower needling his shoulders and neck and easing away the tension of the day. Once he'd dried off and dressed in athletic shorts and a loose-fitting t-shirt, he had rummaged in his kitchen for food. He'd even cussed himself for not thinking to order something the night before at The Black Olive when he was with Bristol. He could have brought home an order of pizza bread or lasagna.

He had finally found a frozen package of pulled barbecued pork, so he'd nuked that enough to defrost it and then dumped it all in a saucepan. He'd eaten two massive sandwiches before Bristol called. By the time he'd gotten off the phone with her, he had been too damned tired to call Taj back.

Rhett reasoned now that if it had been an emergency, Taj would have called back. Or Summer would have called. If it had been something about his parents, someone would have tried harder to get a hold of him.

He'd been thinking about Bristol all day, all over the place with his feelings. When he'd promised her the other night that he would do whatever she wanted or needed until her ex left town, he meant it. But that one kiss was already killing him.

Wasn't like she'd popped up on her toes and given him a quick peck on the lips. A cute little kiss on the cheek. Nope. Bristol had gone all in—she would make a great actress—and pressed her mouth squarely over his and then used her tongue.

The hell of it was, Rhett's heart had exploded in his chest and his brain and maybe his mouth. As far as he knew, she didn't realize what that kiss had meant to him, but not for lack of enthusiasm on his part. Thankfully, she'd kept enough space between them that the rocket in his jeans hadn't been an issue.

Rhett would do his best to play the part of her boyfriend just long enough for the ex to leave her alone. But he knew as much as he loved it, he already hated it. For one thing, it was damned hard to turn that on and off. Bristol could pull him in to suck his face and walk away easily, but each time she did that, she would take a piece of him with her. And, he hated that Bristol needed him to be her fake boyfriend to protect her from herself. She wasn't scared of Trey; she was scared she would go crawling back to him because she might still love him. Because she still found him attractive. Because she was a sucker for a bad boy with a sob story.

That might make Rhett crazy. He would use the opportunity to show her what a good guy was like, to remind her that guys like Trey were only going to hurt her, but pining way for someone who was still hung up on someone like that would get old fast.

She had told him last night when they talked that she hadn't seen Trey. Rhett had no reason to believe she would lie to him. But he also didn't believe her ex had given up that easily. He would keep an eye out for the guy, but it was hard to do that when he was stuck on a three-twelve shift. Not like she lived too far away; he could and would drive to Rodey to see her tonight.

But what if that made her suspicious?

eleven

. . .

BRISTOL

Bristol stared at Summer for a moment, at first too stunned to even laugh. So, someone had seen her lay that kiss on Rhett, someone besides Trey. Any of the employees at the Skeleton Bar, could have been Pierce—he was standing out at the bar with Trey.

"Well?" Summer shrugged as she leaned closer to the table. "Is it true?"

Finally, Bristol snorted softly, and when Summer leaned closer still, expecting some big, juicy secret, she threw her head back and laughed.

"No?" Summer asked. "What? C'mon, girl! Give it up! What's going on?"

Bristol pressed her lips together, trying to hold the laughter inside. She took a drink, shook her head, and finally met Summer's eyes.

"No."

"No." Summer flopped back in her seat. "No, you didn't kiss Rhett Bailey?"

"Well, I did, but no."

Summer eyed her suspiciously.

"I kissed him. Yes." Bristol laughed again. "But it didn't mean anything."

"I heard it was like you guys were burning down the bar."

With a head shake, Bristol arched her eyebrows in disbelief.

"No." She laughed and sipped at her drink again. "No. I mean. I guess it was a hot kiss. But it didn't mean anything."

She should probably be telling Summer it meant everything. If she was going to fake date Rhett Bailey, then she should be selling it to everyone, Summer included. But she couldn't lie to her friend. Not to mention, she trusted Summer to keep the secret, should Trey Kennedy come poking around for information.

"I'm so confused." Summer squeezed her eyes closed and rubbed her fingertips over her forehead. "Is this pregnancy brain?"

"It's a long story."

"Fill me in?"

Bristol sighed as she settled into her chair to get comfortable.

"The guy I told you about? Trey?"

"The fath—"

"You have to stop saying words like that," Bristol insisted. "No one knows but you and me. We can't talk about it, because that's gonna make it easier for one of us to slip and mention it."

"Why would that be so bad?"

"Summer—"

"No, really, answer me. I have no intention of telling anyone. But we're your family here, Bristol. My family. Taj's family. No one's going to judge you for what happened."

Bristol licked her lips. "Maybe so, but it would invite a lot of questions. You have questions. Your mom would have questions." With a shrug, she shook her head, feeling a little desperate. "I don't want to talk about it. And mostly, I don't want it to get back to Trey."

The look on Summer's face said she wanted to argue, but to Bristol's relief, she simply nodded.

"So. Trey."

Summer nodded as Bristol continued.

"He showed up at the Skeleton Bar Thursday night."

"Come again?"

"Yeah. Rhett and I had plans. He walked in close to five. I went back to get my things, and when I came out, ready to leave with Rhett, Trey Kennedy was sitting at the bar."

Summer opened and closed her mouth a couple of times before finally shaking her head.

"Yeah, I don't know. I wasn't trying to hide from him, but also, I didn't particularly want him to show up here, either."

"Did he hurt you?"

"No." Bristol flipped her hair off her shoulders. "He was a lover. Never violent. If he was angry, he would just get sullen and passive aggressive."

"Has he called you? Have you talked to him? Since you've been here?"

"No."

"And it's been almost two years?"

"Right." Bristol nodded. "When I left, I changed cell providers and changed my number. Apparently, Becca told him I'd moved here."

Summer flinched. "Because she didn't know not to."

"Yeah. I want to be mad at her, but I can't. I told my parents, told Bec, that I was leaving for the job opportunity. That Trey and I were going our separate ways. So it's not like she did anything wrong."

"Weird that he would come looking for you after all this time has passed."

Bristol shrugged. "That's what he does, though. He's a drifter. He does odd jobs, but his family has money. He's very charming. And he's like a chameleon. He can change to fit in anywhere."

"So. Where does that kiss come in then?"

Bristol hesitated. She glanced at the door of French Kiss coffee again. Watched a young family walk by, all of them carrying and eating slices of pie from Minnie's Pie Shop. Reminded of old times with her parents and her sister, Bristol felt a faint smile shape her lips.

"Because as much as I didn't want to see him there." She pressed her lips together and drew in a breath deep enough to flare her nostrils. "I wanted to melt when I did."

"You still love him?" Summer asked quietly. "After all this time? After what he did?"

"No." Bristol shook her head the slightest bit. "But I *could* fall again. I know him. And I know *me.* And I know it could happen. And if I'm alone with him, it could happen fast."

"Even knowing he's bad news?"

"Haven't you ever loved a bad boy, Summer?"

twelve

. . .

BRISTOL

Bristol didn't mind Sundays, not like some people did. Maybe that was because she loved her job; being at the Skeleton Bar was more like hanging out with friends and family than working. She didn't sit around on Sundays, anxious or frustrated about having to go back to work the following day. She didn't get to spend many Sundays with Rhett, since his usual schedule was twelve-hour days on the weekends. Although, now and then, they hung out after his shifts ended on the weekends.

Today, though, she was too antsy to hang out at her place alone. She'd done her laundry and cleaned her little rental house by noon. Being a rental, she didn't have to do yard work, so she was bored out of her mind by one. Any given Sunday, she watched whatever sport was on TV, though she preferred football. She liked to read, so if the weather was tolerable, she spent time on her little patio with a book.

She couldn't get lost in anything today. The Cincinnati Reds weren't on TV; she could watch the Braves play if she wanted to. Two innings passed before she realized she wasn't paying any attention. It was sticky outside; her five-minute stroll around her yard to water her plants left her sweaty tank top plastered to her chest. Definitely wouldn't be comfortable to sit outside.

If she hadn't just seen Summer the day before, she might have called her friend. But she didn't want to bug Summer when she was with Taj, not when they'd spent a couple of hours together yesterday, catching up and talking about the one thing Bristol could not get off her mind right now.

Trey Kennedy.

Summer didn't get it. Summer didn't understand the way Trey Kennedy pulled women in and held them captive in his aura, his charm. Bristol wasn't even sure she would call it charm; sure, the guy could meld into any situation. If he hung out at the Skeleton Bar for any length of time, he would fit right in. He and Pierce would talk like they had known each other forever. The Lockland brothers would like him. Erin and Tara—two of the younger waitresses at the bar—would love him. That thought made Bristol flinch. Not out of jealousy, but worry. Tara would be just the kind of woman Trey would put the moves on; she would fall for him in a heartbeat.

Bristol had eventually opened up the flood gates yesterday and talked about all the things she hadn't wanted to say about Trey. She had shared memories with Summer [illegible] told her about the highway driving with Trey, the sunroof open on his car and a sky full of stars above them. Journey music playing. The times they would sit outside in their backyard, also under the stars, and share a bottle of wine. Laying together on a blanket. Soft music playing on their portable speaker.

They hadn't gone out often. When Summer asked what they did for fun, Bristol had stammered, not sure what to say.

Because fun had been those late nights driving with the sunroof open. Or drinking wine. Making love on Sunday afternoons—when Trey was around. And when Summer pressed her, suggested that the whole relationship was about sex, Bristol had agreed.

With the space, the distance, she had finally put between them, Bristol could see that her relationship with Trey had been a lie. He had swept her off her feet, charmed his way into her bed, and continued to blind her with that intense devotion. Trey wasn't her first lover, but he was the first real man she'd been with. He had dazzled her, so much so that she'd been willing to look the other way every time he walked out the door.

"That's not love," Summer had whispered. "Bristol, you deserve more than that."

"I know." Bristol nodded. "Which is why I left."

"You haven't been with anyone since you left him, have you?"

"Nope."

Bristol shuddered now at the memory of the conversation with Summer. It wasn't a big deal. Summer would never share her secrets. But still. Something about baring herself, sharing those secrets and sharing her naiveté with anyone bothered her.

And yet, Bristol needed Summer's help. Yes, she had told Trey she was dating Rhett, and Rhett had told her he would go along with it. But the whole situation was messy, and it would be nice to talk to Summer about it when things got too heavy. Bristol hated using Rhett, but she also knew Trey would still tempt her.

While Rodey had a little fresh market, Kissing Springs had a real grocery store. Bristol decided grocery shopping would be a good way to spend her afternoon. It would keep her busy, and while she had no desire at the moment to cook, later this week, she would be thanking herself.

She listened to the local country station as she drove. Maybe she would invite her sister down to stay with her for a few days soon. This was Becca's last summer before she started college. The two of them could have some fun. Bristol couldn't take her to the revue in Kissing Springs; Becca was too young. But there were plenty of other things they could do. She could even invite her parents down for a weekend; her dad would love to hit the bourbon trail.

Happy to have a few things in mind to busy herself with for the rest of the summer, Bristol was in a much better mood as she strolled the aisles of the store. She bought basics—bread and peanut butter. Apples for herself. Tortilla chips and jarred queso for Rhett because he thought fruit was created by Satan. She teased him about it often—how did he have the palette of a child if he was a nurse? Rhett always argued that most children didn't like basic tortilla chips and spicy queso. They wanted Doritos or Takis.

Bristol chuckled to herself now as she neared the checkout lanes. She put her items on the belt and pulled her billfold from her purse.

"Bristol."

She damned near froze when she heard his voice, but she managed a deep breath and hoped like hell Trey hadn't noticed her moment of panic. Cash in hand as the cashier scanned her items, Bristol looked over her shoulder and offered Trey a smile.

"Hey."

Why was he at the grocery store? In Kissing Springs? If he was traveling, he would be staying in a hotel and eating at restaurants, right?

"How ya doin'?"

Bristol flicked her eyes over the three items in his hands. A bottle of Elijah Craig Toasted, a box of crackers, and a candy bar.

"Good." She nodded. "Is that your lunch? Picnicking?"

With a sheepish grin, Trey ducked his chin to examine his items.

"Busted."

When he tipped his head up to look at her, Summer felt the familiar sting. How many times had she busted him in the short time they were together? Not just with his cheating and running around. Didn't matter that he was ten years her senior, Bristol had mothered him whenever she wasn't naked under his hands.

She handed her cash over when the cashier gave her a total, but she was thinking about Summer. What would her friend say to that revelation?

"Grab lunch with me," he suggested. Summer swallowed down a little thrill, reminding herself he was easy on the eyes, but hard on everything else. His invitation to lunch wasn't a prize for the most interesting girl. He wasn't interested in her; he was interested in a warm body.

"I need to get my groceries home," she argued. Trey set his three things on the conveyor belt and eyed her bags as the cashier put them in her cart.

"There's nothing cold there." He met her eyes with a challenge. "They'll keep in the truck."

Bristol bit her lip. She wished she could argue, but he was right. She wished she could correct him and say she didn't drive a truck anymore. That he didn't know her anymore. But she couldn't do that, either.

"Fine." She shrugged, hoping she sounded more nonchalant than she felt. She waited for him to pay and then walked outside with him. The heat rolled off the asphalt and smacked her in the face as she unlocked her truck and put her bags in the front seat. "Wanna put your stuff in here for now?"

"I'm good." He shook his head, so she swung her door closed and locked it. "There's a diner—"

"Hope's." He cut her off with a nod. "Been there."

"How long have you been in the area?"

"About a week."

That surprised her. Had it taken him that long to find her, or had he been shopping around for other women before showing up at the Skeleton Bar? Not that it mattered. The diner was a short walk, but it felt to Bristol like miles as they trudged through the heat making small talk. The weather wasn't all that different from back home, but they talked it to death. She was sure he wasn't interested in the town history even as she answered his questions. And she knew he didn't give a damn about her parents even though he asked, because he had spent minimal time with them. She supposed it was hard for him to look her parents in the eyes, when he was so much older than her and conspicuously absent at most family functions. Not to mention, her parents hadn't been too excited about her living with him.

"Tell me about your new guy."

It was after lunch time, but well before dinner, so the diner was almost empty. They grabbed a table by the windows.

Bristol picked up the plastic-coated menu even though she knew what she would order. She had the damned thing memorized. But it was better than looking at Trey, because he was burning a hole through her with those intense dark eyes.

thirteen

. . .

RHETT

Rhett was torn between worried and pissed off. He'd called Bristol on his commute from Louisville to Kissing Springs. When she didn't answer, he left her a message asking if she wanted to hang out after he got home. His plan had been to shower and then brown some burger and make tacos. She texted him, instead of calling him back. Not unusual—she might be busy with something. But her answer had simply said *no, not up for it tonight.*

That didn't sound like Bristol, which made him worry. Knowing her ex might still be hanging around town, that she might have seen him, made him worry more. On the other hand, wondering if she'd seen him and spent time with him made Rhett mad.

And that made him mad at himself. He had no rights to dictate what Bristol could or could not do. If anything, they were *fake dating*, and he wasn't sure just how far they would push that—if her ex was around, if she truly wanted her ex to leave her alone, or maybe she just wanted to make him jealous.

That—the idea that she might use Rhett to make her ex jealous—added a whole other layer of pissed off. True, she had no idea how Rhett felt about her, and yes, he'd promised her he had her back where the ex-boyfriend was concerned.

But that didn't mean he had to like being used to make another guy jealous. Nor did he have to like entertaining the idea that Bristol might still have feelings for this guy. That when Rhett was at work, or not with her in Rodey, she could be with Trey. Doing God knows what.

Well, God, and Rhett knew what.

A friend wouldn't be angry about this, not the way it made Rhett angry. Worrying was one thing. No matter what, he didn't want Bristol to get hurt. But, he also wanted her all to himself. She might have kissed him for her own selfish reasons, but Rhett had gone along with it for his selfish reasons, and now he was stuck.

He showered, but he didn't feel like cooking that late just for himself. Instead, he threw on a pair of shorts and a t-shirt and went to his parents' house, hoping to score some leftovers.

"Hey." His mom greeted him with her warm, welcoming smile.

"Hi, Mom." He leaned down just a bit to hug her. Tall and slim, his mother was quite a looker, as his dad used to say. Still said. "I was hoping you had some leftovers."

She backed away with a knowing smile on her face and nodded for him to follow her into the kitchen.

"Where's Bristol?" she asked as she took a plate from the refrigerator, peeled the cling wrap from it, and popped it in the microwave. Rhett wasn't sure he wanted to talk about his friend, not with all this emotional turmoil just under the surface. His mom would sense it. Hell, his parents and his brother—they all knew he had a thing for Bristol Miller. As much time as he spent with the woman, how in the hell did she not see it?

"Busy." He plopped down on a stool and rested his elbows on the kitchen island.

"How was work?"

Relieved Mom had moved right on from the subject of Bristol, he shrugged and took a deep breath. "It was good."

"Good." She nodded. "Tea or lemonade?"

"Tea," he answered. "I can get it, Mom. You don't have to wait on me." He stood, but his mom waved her hand at him dismissively.

"Sit down. You worked all day."

"What's cooking?" He sniffed the air; his stomach growled loud enough that she heard it.

"Roast and carrots and potatoes."

"Oh, man." He nodded his appreciation. "I was going to fix tacos."

Mom smiled as she poured a glass of tea and handed it to him. Rhett drank deeply and watched when she refilled the glass immediately.

"Wanna talk about it?"

"Talk about what?" he asked her.

The microwave beeped, so Mom busied herself with getting the plate for him. She grabbed silverware and a napkin and put both in front of him. Rhett stuck his fork in the roast. So tender, a small chunk came apart. He scooped it into his mouth and groaned.

"Man, I am hungry," he mumbled. "Seems like lunch was a year or two ago."

"Don't talk with your mouth full," she scolded him. He took another bite while she put a kettle of water on the stove to boil.

"You still drink tea to sleep?" he asked her curiously.

"Mm-hmm." She nodded as she rested her back on the counter by the stove. "The older I get, the more elusive a good night's sleep is."

"You're not old," he argued around a mouthful of carrots.

"Rhett Charles." She glared at him with the mom eyes.

This time, he swallowed and wiped his mouth. "Sorry."

"So?" She tipped her head.

"I don't know what you're getting at, Mom." He shook his head as he reached for his tea. "You're gonna have to give me a clue."

"Word around town is that someone saw you and Bristol kissing."

"Huh." Eyes on his plate, Rhett frowned and forked another piece of roast. He wasn't sure how to handle this. He had told Bristol he had her back and would be her fake boyfriend until she no longer needed a fake boyfriend. Presumably, that meant even when he wasn't with her, even with his family and her family and every damned person in Kissing Springs and Rodey, he was still to act the part.

But he didn't want to lie to his mom.

"Is it true?"

"Yep." He nodded. "Who told you? How the hell did Minnie know about it?"

Mom straightened from the counter and glanced at the tea kettle, as if her mom glare would make the water boil faster.

"Taj told me."

"Aww, man." Rhett groaned. "He's totally gonna ride my ass about this now."

"Language." Firm tone and the mom glare again. "Seems like you might deserve it. You gave him a lot of grief before he and Summer got things figured out."

"I gave him a lot of grief because he was taking money to strip down to a cock sock and thrust his hips at women."

"Rhett." She squeezed her eyes closed and pressed her fingertips to the bridge of her nose. "Not a visual I care to have in my head."

"He did it. Not me."

"Tell me about Bristol."

"It's complicated," he mumbled with a lazy shrug.

"I'd think you would be on cloud nine!" She rested her hands on the counter now and watched him clean his plate. "You've been mooning around over her for six months now."

Well, for the duration of the kiss, yes, he had been on cloud nine. No question. Maybe cloud nineteen. But no, being her fake boyfriend wouldn't sustain cloud nine status. In fact, after working all weekend and not seeing her and her cryptic text earlier, he had crashed out of any clouds, and now he was frustrated.

Maybe hurt.

Which was stupid. Because he had told her he was all-in. All he had to do was tell her no. He didn't want to fake date her.

"Rhett?" Mom nudged his hand. He forced a smile when he looked up at her.

"It was a great kiss," he said truthfully. "But I'm not sure where things are going from there."

"What?"

"I mean." He swallowed some tea and shrugged. "Yeah. Yeah, we're goin' out." Play the part, he told himself. Just until her ex was out of her hair. Then they'd have to fake a breakup.

"You don't seem thrilled."

Why did his mom have to be so intuitive?

"I am, Mom," he promised her. "It's just still pretty new. Ya know? Don't want to jinx anything."

"Silly boy." Mom tousled his hair as the tea kettle started whistling. "You can't jinx fate."

He was pretty sure he and Bristol weren't fated to be together. Maybe in his head and heart, but it was painfully obvious she didn't feel the same way about him.

"Right." He nodded when Mom looked back at him. "Thanks. For dinner."

fourteen

. . .

BRISTOL

Rhett hadn't shown up by the time she closed the bar Monday night. She had texted him again last night, after the text turning down his invite to hang out. No details, because she wasn't sure she owed him any, but mostly because she didn't want to end up in a marathon text session with Rhett about her ex.

She simply texted him around ten, apologized for being tired—not the complete truth, but still completely true—and told him she would see him today. If there was one thing she could count on, it was Rhett Bailey showing up at the bar to hang with her for a while. He'd been in and out of the bar so much in the past six months, Bristol sometimes joked that she should give him a key.

And now, she was locking up to leave the place alone. He might be busy; he often helped his dad out around their property. Even with Waylon Bailey retiring recently, there was too much land for him to handle on his own anymore. Rhett worked a full-time schedule at the hospital, but he sometimes put in enough hours with his dad for another full-time job.

Still, it felt weird that he hadn't answered her. If he wasn't coming, if he couldn't get away to see her, he usually sent a text or left her a voicemail. It felt ominous that he'd gone silent after everything that had happened the last several days. Bristol had never told Rhett about Trey; as close as they were —they shared childhood stories and dreams and actual dreams they had when sleeping and talked about work and movies and music—she'd never confided in him about Trey.

Because she'd never confided in anyone about Trey. Except Summer.

Maybe he was angry with her for keeping it from him. Then again, Rhett had never shared any love stories with her. Maybe after having the weekend to think about it, he was mad about her kissing him and didn't want to be her fake boyfriend.

Or maybe he's just busy, she told herself as she pulled her phone from her purse. She liked that it stayed light later during the summer. The walk to her truck was never dangerous; she wasn't afraid to be alone in the lot. But summer nights with the setting sun painting the sky and the chirp of crickets and the possibility of anything fun happening made her feel alive. Always had. Maybe, she mused as she walked to her truck, it was still the athlete in her. She had played fast pitch softball for a travel team every summer from the time she was twelve until she was eighteen. And after that, she'd played slow-pitch with friends back in Indiana, and now she played co-ed with the Locklands' team. She loved summer nights at the ball field.

They played tomorrow. The thought put a little skip in her

step. The tournament Cole was rounding up extra players for would be a blast, too.

"Hey."

She jumped when she heard his voice. Maybe she was a little on edge, after all. But not because she worried about someone dangerous lurking around anywhere in the evenings. Nope. She'd frozen in the store yesterday when Trey spoke to her, and now Rhett had scared her.

"Hey." She flashed him a smile and set her purse and keys on the tailgate of his truck. "What're you doing out here? I thought you weren't coming."

"Decided I didn't want to guzzle beer while I waited." He shrugged and patted the spot beside him. Bristol eyed him curiously as she turned her back to the truck, rested her hands on the gate, and hoisted herself up to sit by him.

"You know you don't have to order anything when you come in. Right?" She stared straight ahead, hating that it felt weird to talk to Rhett. Even after they'd gone out for pizza the other night, it felt weird to sit here with him after kissing him and then not seeing him for three days.

"Yep."

From the corner of her eye, she saw him nod and then hold something out to her. She looked down and smiled when she saw the candy bar in his hand.

"If you don't need to guzzle beer, maybe I don't need candy bars all the time."

Rhett shrugged and took it back. "Suit yourself."

She laughed softly.

"I haven't been here long." He tore the wrapper open and took a bite. Bristol inhaled the scent of chocolate and wished she hadn't said anything.

"How was your weekend?" she asked him.

"Good." He nodded and offered the candy bar to her again. "Wanna bite?"

"I do." She laughed as she leaned over and wrapped her hand around his to take a bite. "You know me too well."

She was joking, but in light of everything that had happened the last few days, it didn't sound that funny. Rhett stared at her silently for a moment before looking away.

"So." He cleared his throat. "My mom asked about us."

Bristol flinched and gave him a curt nod.

"Wasn't sure how to handle that one, Bristol. I mean, I figured the fewer people who know this isn't real, the better. So I didn't tell her otherwise."

"Okay."

"You tell me. If you think he'll ride off into the sunset anytime soon, we'll clear things up."

"I wish," she whispered as she leaned back to rest on her hands. She tipped her head up to study the sky, but it was much too early to wish on stars.

"What do you mean?"

"I had lunch with him yesterday." She shook her head. "Unfortunately, he's not going anywhere soon."

"Why'd you have lunch with him?" He shot her a frown. "I thought you were trying to avoid him."

"I was. I am." She shrugged helplessly. "But I was at the grocery store. Saw him there. He asked me to have lunch."

"Where'd you go?"

"Hmm?" She dragged her gaze from the sky to look at him. "Hope's Diner."

"And?"

"Nothing." She shook her head. "I mean, we talked for a bit. He's…he's in a VRBO on Daisy Drive. Hanging out for a while to see if he likes the vibe here."

"Doesn't this guy work?" Rhett sounded grouchy.

"When we lived together, he worked in sales. The beverage industry. But, his mom's family has money. He likes to spend it."

She stared at Rhett, watched him stare toward the bar and the gift shop.

"Did he ask about us?"

"Yeah. He did." She leaned forward and swung her legs like a little girl.

"So, should we maybe talk about the details?" Rhett shrugged and peeked at her before looking back at the buildings. "If he's gonna be around, and we have to act like we're involved, we should probably have our stories straight."

"We should." She nodded. "Okay. Um, I told him we met about six months ago. True enough."

"True *enough*? What? We did meet six months ago."

She grinned and continued, "And that we started dating about three months ago."

"That's it?"

"Well, if we were really dating, I don't think I'd have given him any more information than that."

"Good point."

"But I guess, we should make up some stuff in case anyone else asks. In case it gets back to him."

"Who would tell him about us?"

"Trust me. If he's still here in a week or two, your mom and dad will roll out the red carpet and serve him the fatted calf for dinner."

"Was that a Biblical reference?" Rhett tipped his head and narrowed his eyes at her.

"Yeah, it was," she snorted. "But it's true."

"Pretty sure you're wrong," he answered. "Did your parents like him?"

"Well, not really, but then what parents would like a guy ten years older than their daughter shacking up with her?"

"Ten years—?" Rhett groaned and shook his head. "That's awful, Bristol. I mean, how did he—? How—?"

"Rhett, I was twenty-two when we started seeing each other. That made him thirty-two. Not so ancient, huh?"

Rhett laughed softly. "No, but still. I hate thinking of you with him."

fifteen

. . .

RHETT

“Maybe we should talk about us.”

Bristol’s whisper was thick with an emotion Rhett couldn’t identify if he wanted to. He didn’t. Want to. Because odds were, she was upset about the ex. Rhett, as a guy, didn’t fit into this equation at all.

He was Bristol’s friend. Didn’t matter how much he wished things were different, Bristol had never given him reason to think or hope otherwise.

“Okay.” He nodded. “Like what?”

“Well, have we gone out on our first date?” She tipped her head as she looked at him. She was still leaning forward, swinging her legs. With her dark hair pulled up in a loose twist and a touch of makeup on her eyes, she looked innocent and carefree.

Rhett flinched and looked away. He had to stop thinking like this. She wasn’t innocent, and she didn’t have to be. Maybe that's not what he meant, though. She looked cute. Almost flirty.

Wishful thinking.

Dammit, Rhett.

"Hey." She elbowed him in the side. "You okay?"

"Yeah, trying to decide what we did on our first date."

"Well, I mean, to narrow it down, there aren't a lot of options around here. Unless you took me to a ball game in Louisville."

Rhett jerked his gaze around to look at her. "Would you wanna go to a game?"

"Like." She frowned. "If we were really dating, would I want to go? Is that what you mean? Are you trying to make it believable?"

Nope. Not what he meant at all. He could take her to a Louisville Bats game. Just as friends. But it was probably better to concentrate on their fake relationship right now so they got details squared away.

"We need to make it real," he reminded her. "And you like softball."

"Yeah." She nodded enthusiastically. "That would work."

"Okay, so we went to a game."

"But what date?"

"Do we have to be that specific?" He shook his head. "No one I know is gonna demand the date so they can go look up the schedule."

"True."

"Would he?"

"No."

Rhett wouldn't swear to it, but it felt like Bristol was avoiding eye contact.

"That's probably all we need to say for sure, right? First date was at a Bats game."

"Well, we are together all the time," he reminded her. "So yeah, I don't think it would be too much of a jump for anyone to believe we're seeing each other. And anything else probably falls outside of things we would normally share, right?"

She nodded. "Speaking of which…"

"Speaking of what?" he asked her. She still seemed distant. She had stopped swinging her legs, and now she sat completely still, her gaze locked on the woods out behind the Lockland land.

"I had coffee with Summer Saturday morning," she told him.

"You told me that."

"She asked me about the kiss."

"Oh." He nodded. "That explains how Taj knew."

"Taj knows?"

"He's the one who told Mom."

Bristol hissed and hung her head. "I'm sorry."

"For what?"

"For your family thinking you're involved with me." She shrugged. "For asking you to lie to your family."

"Not a big deal," he promised her. He hooked his arm around her neck and reeled her in. "We'll let everyone think we're dating, and then when you're ready, we'll tell everyone we broke up."

"We won't have to pretend to hate each other, will we?" she asked with a smirk.

"No. We'll just tell them there's no chemistry. That we're just good friends."

"Right." She nodded. "Kill the lie with the truth, right?"

Well, that stung. Rhett nodded. "Yeah. Right. Whatever it takes to keep the creep away from you."

"He's not a creep," Bristol argued softly.

"He is to me, if he was hitting on you when you were barely legal to drink."

She sighed and leaned her head on his chin.

"Agree to disagree."

"I'm not asking the world to hate him," Rhett promised her. "I just don't want him around you. You're different now that he's around, and I want my friend Bristol back."

She nodded as he released her to sit up straight.

"You ready for the game tomorrow night?" He tapped her foot with his, happy it set her in motion again. Grin on her face, legs swinging, she nodded.

"Yes. I'm ready for the tournament!"

"The one Summer is *not* playing in?"

"For fuck's sake, Rhett Bailey." She laughed and elbowed him more aggressively.

"Is that one fuck or more than one?" When she looked at him, he gave her an innocent shrug. "Serious question."

"I think it's for the sake of all the fucks," she answered after a second. "But whatever it is, we are not getting into that discussion again. It's between Summer and Taj."

'That's true."

"You're agreeing with me?" She turned her head and eyed him suspiciously.

"Sheridan said she's free," he announced. "So, that's one more body on the roster."

"Name."

"Hmm?"

"Name. Name on the roster."

Rhett rolled his eyes. "What time do you get off work?"

"Leaving around four-thirty. The game's at six?"

"Yeah."

"I'll be there." She hopped off the gate of his truck and gave him a nod. "Starting on shortstop."

"Whatever you need to tell yourself to sleep at night."

"See ya tomorrow, Rhett."

sixteen

. . .

BRISTOL

She wasn't surprised when she saw Trey sitting on the bleachers. Not when she saw him talking and laughing with Branch Lockland. Not when Branch extended his arm and apparently introduced him to his parents—Jolene and Harlan. They would love him, too. Unless Bristol decided to be petty and marched over to them now and told them just a sliver of her and Trey's story. Then they would be considerably less friendly with him. They weren't rude; they wouldn't treat him badly. But they were protective, and the whole family had taken Bristol in as one of their own.

The only thing that surprised her was Trey in shirt sleeves. He usually wore a denim jacket, even when it was ninety degrees in the shade. In dark wash jeans and a pristine white t-shirt, he looked like a male model waiting on a photo shoot to start. His tousled, messy curls begged for a woman's fingers to tangle in them. Bristol flexed her fingers, completely unaware of the movement.

"You're staring," Summer told her.

Bristol shook her head. "Nah. Just kind of fascinating to watch him weave his spell over everyone."

"They might be polite, but you know they've got—"

"I know." She nodded and glanced at Summer. "Are you playing?"

"No." Summer shook her head. "You guys have enough tonight, so I'm cheering you on."

"Cool."

"How're things with Rhett?"

"Good." Bristol looked around, curious about the warm flutter in her belly when she saw Rhett out on the field with Cole and Taj. He wore denim well; most of the guys around here did. But Bristol had to admit, she didn't hate seeing some of them in shorts, too. Rhett had nice, muscular thighs, almost like she would expect on a soccer player. He had a cute butt, too, but she would never tell him that. They all wore the same forest green t-shirt with the Lockland Distilling logo on the front and a number on the back. Rhett was number eleven. Bristol was number four, the same number she'd been all through her travel team, high school, and college years.

"Yeah?" Summer smirked at her. "You guys going out after the game?"

Bristol blinked at her friend and decided she was talking louder on purpose. Time to perpetuate the myth, she decided.

"Yeah, maybe."

"'kay. I'm gonna go sit." Summer leaned in close as she slipped by Bristol. "Taj thinks you guys are really going out."

Bristol nodded, relieved that Summer hadn't told him the truth. It would be hard to fool everyone else if Rhett's big brother didn't act like he believed in the lie. Best to keep him in the dark. Branch cut through the pregame chatter with a shrill whistle. Bristol tossed her glove on the bench and wandered out to the field to join the team circle.

"Number seven," Branch was saying. "Fucking kills the ball. No girls on the infield when he's at bat."

Bristol might have argued, but she saw the look of warning on Rhett's face. Instead, she nodded along with the rest of the women on the team.

"And number twelve? That chick's faster than a cheetah," Branch continued. "She gets on, she's gonna shoot for a double, even if it's a shallow fly ball dropped."

"Who's gonna drop a shallow fly ball?" Cole asked his brother.

"You did two games ago," Branch reminded him.

"Dude, I left two inches of skin on the field trying to snow cone that ball."

Branch shrugged as if to say *but you didn't, did you?*

"I busted my—"

"Guys." Knox shook his head. "Seriously. Grow up, Cole. Branch, I think we all know what we're doing here, right?"

Bristol snorted softly. Rhett's sister Sheridan caught her eye and grinned. At the same time, they mouthed the word *men* and then burst into laughter. Branch gave them both the evil eye, but they huddled up, hands in the center, to get the game going.

"Whiskey on three!" Branch looked at each of them. Bristol stared back, ready to go. Branch counted them off, and like the ragtag group they were, they yelled *whiskey* but not particularly in unison. Good thing they were better ball players than cheerleaders.

"Bristol, you're lead-off," Knox called. Bristol reached for her bat, confused when she didn't find it parked against the fence where she'd left it.

"Looking for this?"

She jumped when the cold aluminum touched the inside of her thighs. Everyone laughed, including Bristol, when she turned to see Rhett with an ornery grin on his face. He goosed her again with the bat before she snatched it out of his hands.

"Start us off, hot stuff."

To her utter shock, he leaned over and dropped a quick kiss on her parted lips. No tongue, but she felt his warm breath over her open mouth. Knox and Branch Lockland cut loose with more shrill whistles. Bristol's cheeks were on fire as she stepped onto the field, bat in her hands. She took a few practice swings and then turned her attention to the team on the field. Wearing red t-shirts, they repped Holmes Liquor Mart. There weren't many local teams, so Branch's scouting report wasn't necessary. They had played these guys a few times already this summer, so they all had the scoop.

"Batter up!"

Bristol grinned at Tom Goldstein, the behind the plate umpire. He was a regular at the Skeleton. She stepped into the batter's box, got comfortable, and rested her bat on her shoulder.

"Let's go, Bristol!"

Her teammates yelled from the bench and their families and friends cheered from the bleachers. But the one voice Bristol heard was Rhett's. She took the first pitch for a ball, outside.

The second pitch was a meatball, so despite the one and oh count, she attacked the ball and connected for a line drive over the second baseman's head. Sheridan, coaching first, gave her five when she had rounded first and come back to stand with her left foot touching the bag.

"Nice hit."

"Thanks."

"Are you dating my brother?"

Bristol laughed softly and peeked at Rhett's sister. Cole stepped into the batter's box.

"Yeah, I am."

Cole drove the first pitch for a long foul down left field line.

"Are you sleeping with my brother?"

Bristol turned to look at Sheridan with wide eyes. "What?"

"Are you?"

"No." She shook her head, but when Sheridan gave her a frown, she added, "not yet."

seventeen

• • •

RHETT

"I can't believe she said she'd go out with you."

"Don't be a dick, man." Rhett shot Taj a frown as they trotted out to the field together.

"I mean, you're ugly, but then I am taken."

Rhett drove his elbow into Taj's side just before they separated for their positions. Taj peeled off to go to left field, Rhett would play left center—just behind Bristol at shortstop. When he played high school baseball, he was the starting shortstop. He was good; Bristol might be better. She had good range, and she had a damned good arm. But he still hated seeing her on the infield when particular guys came up to bat.

The trouble was, she wouldn't leave a line drive or a ground ball alone. She was too good with her glove, and she hated to let something get by, even if it might save her pretty face.

He did like playing behind her, though. Easy on the eyes, watching her lithe body move around her position. When she was ready, she stayed low, which put her sweet little ass out there on display. Probably Rhett's favorite, although he loved to see her short hop a ground ball and throw a frozen rope to first for the out.

Funny. The league was recreational, but some of them were pretty competitive, including himself and Bristol. First inning, and her left leg was already dusty from her hip down over her gray ball pants to her cleats. She had tagged at third to score on Knox's fly ball, but it was a close play at the plate, so naturally, she slid. That was why she wore ball pants instead of shorts. Rhett would slide in shorts, if he needed to, but he understood Bristol didn't want to.

She peeked at him over her shoulder now. Rhett laughed, the memory of her jumping when he goosed her with her bat front and center in his mind. It wasn't real, but he liked the game they were playing. He liked having the okay to say flirty things to her and to drop a kiss on her when she least expected it. He would pay for it. Eventually, her ex would find someone new to bother or better yet, just move away completely, and Bristol wouldn't need a fake boyfriend anymore. But Rhett was all in until that time came.

"Play's at one!" Branch hollered from third base. Rhett watched Bristol wander over closer to Branch and say something to make him laugh. Her dark hair was pulled back in a long French braid, which always made Rhett want to nibble on her neck, even more so now that he knew he could do it and she wouldn't care.

The umpire called for a batter and the bottom of the first inning began. Rhett noticed Bristol's ex talking to Summer's mom and dad. They all appeared to be having a good time. He supposed Bristol was right; as much as he hated to admit it, his parents would probably like him, too. Until he gave them the scoop.

The leadoff batter flew out to right field. The second batter hit a hard ground ball at Branch who scooped it up and threw the guy out no problem. Bristol fived Branch as she returned to her position; she'd automatically moved to back him up on the off chance the ball would get by him. With two outs, the next batter singled to right center. Pierce, the bartender, could probably have thrown her out at first, but he only ran the ball in, eyes on the runner.

Bristol had told Rhett one thing she missed about fast pitch was stealing. She wished stealing bases was a thing in slow pitch. Now that they had a runner on first, she gave him a look from her spot on shortstop. Rhett grinned and nodded, knowing she was saying she would have the throw if the runner could steal.

When the inning ended with no runs scored, they trotted back off the field together. Bristol snatched a bottle of Gatorade from the bench and took the lid off. Rhett watched her tip her head back for a long swallow. Sweat dampened her hair line, and her cheeks were rosy with heat and sunshine. She looked seventeen, except for her sweet little curves in all the right places.

Without looking at him, she handed him her bottle so he could take a drink. He chugged half of it before handing it back to her.

"Seriously?" She took it back and gave him a dirty look.

"Sorry." He leaned down to kiss her cheek.

"Get a room, people!" Pierce yelled from where he stood to coach third base.

"Yeah," Knox decided to throw in his two cents. He stood at the end of the dugout, arms crossed over his chest. "When did this even start?"

"It's been a while," Rhett said quietly, feeling Bristol watching him. "We just kept it quiet for a bit."

"Really?" Sheridan asked from her spot at the fence. Fingers wound through the fence to hold on, she looked at Rhett over her shoulder. "I thought Bristol was smarter than that."

"Says the only single Bailey sibling." Rhett winked at her.

"Hey, I'm lookin' out for Bristol," Sheridan argued as she turned back to the field. "Let's go Tara! Base hit!"

Bristol inched closer to the fence, eyes on the game. Rhett was content to watch her, but he was on deck, so he grabbed a bat and kept it to himself this time. While he now had permission to flirt and be goofy with her, he didn't want to take advantage of that and be a dick. Bristol watched him step into the on-deck circle and swing his bat.

"Wanna go out later?" he asked her. "Grab a burger at the Iron Stag?"

"Yeah." She nodded immediately. "Sounds good."

Tara took a walk. Rhett grabbed her bat and handed it back to Marlow Dailey, who was up after him. But he was still looking at Bristol.

And she was watching him with a cute little smirk on her face.

eighteen

. . .

BRISTOL

Half the team decided to go to the Iron Stag after the game. Trey too, at Pierce and Tara's invitations. Caught up in the fun of the game—the ball game and the game she was playing with Rhett—Bristol only took a second to be angry that Trey would be tagging along with them.

In the parking lot, at the passenger door of Rhett's truck, she kicked off her cleats and stepped into her comfortable sporty slides.

"That was fun." Rhett came up behind her and trapped her between the open door and the cab of the truck. Bristol shivered when she felt his lips brush the back of her neck.

"It was," she agreed. "Nice triple."

Rhett backed off and offered her a smile when she turned her head to look at him.

"How come Summer didn't play?"

"Because we didn't need her," she answered easily. "They're going to the Iron Stag, though."

Rhett nodded and rested his hand on her hip to spin her around to face him.

"Good." He took a moment to look at her, eyes marking every streak of dirt she imagined she wore on her face. She loved that he was this prepared to protect her, to pretend for her, but something about having her best friend look at her so intensely made her want to squirm. "Ready?"

"Mm-hmm." Her heart hammered a few stutter beats when she thought he was going to kiss her again. What was that about? She wasn't embarrassed. Well, not embarrassed to be seen with Rhett Bailey, but yes, their friends were going to tease them relentlessly about dating, about taking forever to get together, taking forever to tell anyone, and anticipating the teasing made her a little anxious.

Rhett dropped his arms from where he had propped them again on the door and the cab of the truck and backed away from her. Bristol climbed into the passenger seat as he hopped up into the driver's seat.

"Branch had a helluva play at third," Rhett mumbled as he started the truck. Bristol nodded her agreement. Branch had taken a throw from Tara in right field and laid down a perfect tag. But the runner had come in hard; even though he slid, he nearly took Branch out. The runner managed to take Branch's legs out from under him and knock him backwards, but Branch held on to the ball and held the tag for the out.

If it had been Bristol covering on third on that throw, she would probably have gotten hurt. She knew it just as well as Rhett knew if she had covered third, she would have stood right in there and taken the same abuse Branch had.

"Um." She cleared her throat as Rhett pulled out of the gravel parking lot and sped off down the highway.

"What?"

"Your sister asked me if we're sleeping together."

"Nice, Sheridan." He rolled his eyes.

"I just told her not yet."

"Well, if you decide to tell her we have, give me the head's up."

"I will."

"Make me sound like a real stud, wouldja?"

Bristol snorted and dropped her head back to rest on the truck seat. "Of course, Rhett. Want me to make up details?"

"No." He shuddered at the thought. "No. My sister does not need to know anything. Just that I blew you away."

"Got it."

Bristol spotted Taj's truck when Rhett pulled into the lot. Struck with relief and nerves, too, she hesitated when Rhett parked and shut the engine off. She was happy Summer was here; she was comfortable with Summer, and it helped that she knew the truth. But Taj was going to be merciless in his teasing.

"You okay?"

Bristol glanced at Rhett with a nod and a small smile. "I'm good."

She pushed her door open thinking how much fun it would be if she and Rhett were actually dating. Well, not she and Rhett, but how much fun it would be to be involved with someone and be close with his family and friends. The thought took her by surprise. She had been telling herself since she moved here that she wasn't ready to date anyone. Not because she was waiting on Trey to come and find her. Just because the whole thing with Trey was a letdown, and she wanted all that disappointment gone. She wanted to find her peace, her happiness, within herself before thinking about dating again.

Rhett pulled the door open for her and leaned in to kiss her as she walked by him. Bristol laughed softly as she patted his cheek and stepped into the bar. The smell of fried foods hit her instantly, making her stomach rumble.

Taj stood at the bar talking to the bartender. Marlowe, their first baseman, usually tended bar at the Iron Stag, but James filled in when she played ball. Bristol looked around for Summer and headed her way when she saw her seated at a couple of tables pushed together.

"Nice game." Summer winked at her as she dropped into a chair across the table from her. The wink suggested Summer was talking about Rhett and not the ball game. Bristol leaned in to rest her elbows on the table and laughed as she covered her face with her hands.

"This is crazy." She peeked at Summer from behind her hands and then dropped them to the table. "Sheridan asked me if I'm sleeping with him."

"I'm just gonna tell you Taj Bailey has a nice body," Summer said with a smirk. "I would imagine Rhett does, too."

"You can tell that by looking." Bristol shook her head. She watched Rhett at the bar now with his brother. The seat of his shorts was covered in dust like he hadn't thought to brush it away after sliding into home in the fifth inning. Maybe she'd take care of it for him when he came over to the table. The thought made her face burn.

"What'd you tell Sheridan?"

Bristol jerked her gaze from her fake boyfriend's ass to meet Summer's eyes. "Just said not yet."

"For what it's worth," Summer hedged with a dramatic shrug.

"I'm not going to sleep with him!" Bristol rolled her eyes. "We're just friends."

"Well." Summer sipped from a water glass, attention on the door now. Bristol turned to see Sheridan, Pierce, and Tara walk in with Trey on their heels. "Seems like your ex likes Kentucky. Either you're gonna be stuck with Rhett for a while, or you might need to find Trey Kennedy a woman."

"I wouldn't do that to another woman." Bristol looked back at Summer. "Rhett's not so bad to be stuck with."

"And all I'm saying is you should get all the perks of being—"

"What's goin' on?"

Bristol and Summer looked up as Sheridan pulled the chair next to Bristol out and plopped down to sit. In deference to the heat, she had shoved her shirt sleeves up over her shoulders. Sweat and dirt caked her face in a few spots. Blood dripped from her knee all the way down to her dirty socks.

"How's the knee?" Bristol tipped her head trying to get a look at Sheridan's strawberry. She dove for a short fly ball in right center field, making the out but tearing up the knee she landed on.

Sheridan shrugged. "Kinda hurts."

"Nothing a shot of Lockland won't cure," Summer told her.

"Agreed." Sheridan nodded. "I love that I moved back from Arizona. Just perfect timing, too."

"Yeah? Did you play ball in high school?"

"I did, but that's not what I meant." Sheridan shook her head in answer to Bristol's question. "I'm glad Summer and Taj asked me to play, but I just meant I'm so glad I moved back to meet the two women who whipped my brothers into shape."

"Rhett's still a work in process," Bristol said quietly. She certainly hadn't whipped him into shape.

"Yeah, so's Taj, honestly," Summer answered. The three of them laughed together.

"When did you and Rhett start dating?" Sheridan asked her.

"Do not badger my girlfriend for any sexy none-of-your-business details!" Rhett approached the table with a pitcher of beer and a stack of plastic cups.

"I just asked when you guys started dating!" Sheridan held her hands up as if to say she was innocent.

"It's been a little bit, but it's still kind of new," Rhett told his sister as he leaned over Summer to set the pitcher down. "So, we kept it quiet for a while."

"And came out of the gate hard," Sheridan told him. "Kissing her in the dugout isn't exactly low key."

"I'm guessing he came out hard," Summer mumbled. Sheridan held her hand up for a high five. Bristol ducked her blushing face and laughed when Summer slapped Sheridan's hand.

"Want something to eat?" Rhett had come around the table to stand behind her. He rested his hands on her shoulders and gave her a gentle squeeze.

"Yes. My stomach is growling."

"Cheeseburger?"

"Yes, please."

"Fries?" he asked.

Sheridan turned to Bristol with a serious frown. "I'd suggest fries over onion rings."

Summer snorted and held her hand up for Sheridan to give her five.

"Oh my God." Bristol groaned. She elbowed Sheridan in the ribs. "Time to find you someone next."

"No." Sheridan shook her head as Rhett wandered back to the bar to order their food. "You know, I'm gettin' old. My boobs are starting to sag. I've put on weight. Pregnancy is a risk when you get closer to forty. Maybe I don't need a guy."

Bristol glanced at Summer with a frown.

"You're in your mid-thirties."

Sheridan shrugged and waved her hand up and down her chest as if presenting it for evidence.

"Are you, like, fishing for compliments?" Bristol tipped her head. "You have great boobs, woman. Stop complaining."

Sheridan laughed as she reached for the stack of cups. "Eh. I just get so tired of the whole thing. The dating. And trying to get to know someone. And the trust thing is a pain."

"Tell me about it," Bristol mumbled.

"You don't trust Rhett?" Sheridan pulled the cups apart and then began filling each from the pitcher.

"I trust Rhett with my life," Bristol answered sincerely. "My ex was a serial cheater."

"Ah." Sheridan nodded. "See? That's what I mean."

"Bristol."

She looked up quickly when Taj hollered at her from across the bar.

"Rhett's got some dirt on his butt. Can you take care of that for him?"

nineteen

• • •

RHETT

"Uncle Rhett!" Stella yelled as he climbed down out of his truck. Rhett swung the door closed and watched his youngest niece gallop over the yard on her stick horse. "What're you doin' here?"

"Came just to see you and Ellery Bean," Rhett told her. "And Rosie," he added when Stella tipped her head at him and gave him the evil eye. At the mention of her stick horse's name, she beamed. Even batted her eyelashes at him. Rhett snorted softly, wondering if she picked that up from her mother—his ex-sister-in-law—or Summer.

"Stell—Oh, hey, Rhett." Summer stepped out the front door of Taj's house. Rhett mentally corrected himself; Summer was living with his brother now. They hadn't talked about marriage in anything other than very nondescript generalized ways, but Rhett knew his brother. Taj was head over heels in love with Summer Lockland, despite trying hard not to be when they first started seeing each other. "Whatcha doing?"

Rhett and Stella crossed the yard, Stella back on Rosie. Taj had been a rodeo champion when he was younger, but injuries had taken their toll on his body. And his ex-wife, then girlfriend, announced she was pregnant. Taj had stepped up, married Marley, and got a real job, but Marley burned through his savings and then found herself a new sugar daddy.

While Rhett wasn't one to talk about people when they weren't around to defend themselves, he wasn't a fan of Marley. The only good thing to come from his brother's marriage to her was this little spitfire beside him and her big sister, Ellery. He eyed Stella as they approached the porch where Summer stood. The little girl dropped Rosie at Summer's feet and wrapped her chubby little arms around her legs.

"Just came by to say hi," he told Summer.

"Nice." She nodded. "Want some lemonade?"

"Yes."

"Grab Rosie, Stel," Summer told Stella as she turned back to pull the screen door open again. Taj's house—*Summer and Taj's house*—was very small. Not a tiny house as Marley liked to call it when she had an ax to grind with Taj. But it was small, and adding Summer and another baby was going to make for tight quarters. Taj had mentioned that he and Summer planned to add on, making space for the older girls to have their own rooms.

Stella grabbed Rosie the stick horse from the porch and hurried inside ahead of them. Rhett liked that Summer didn't belittle Stella for having the wild imagination to pretend that Rosie was real and that Stella wanted to be in the rodeo one day. Marley had done her best to squelch any discussion, pretend or not, about rodeo and make believe.

"Taj is out back," Summer announced when they were in the kitchen. "He's got the lot marked up back there for the addition."

"Really?" Rhett watched her pour two glasses of lemonade. "That's great. I told him I'd help him."

She nodded. "Well, I mean, marking it off isn't a big deal. I'm sure he'd like your help when he starts building."

Rhett thanked her when she handed him a glass.

"So." She set the pitcher back in the refrigerator and slumped against the closed door to study him. "How are you?"

"Good."

"Summer, can I go outside with Daddy?"

Summer glanced at Stella with a smile. "Yes. But don't get in Daddy's way, okay?"

"Will you come out, too, Uncle Rhett?"

"I'll be there in a minute," he promised her. "Where's Ellery?"

"Playdate with a friend," Summer answered.

"Oh. Poor Stella."

Summer laughed and nodded at the table behind him. He had walked by without noticing the books spread open and a set of watercolors in the middle of the table.

"We were painting. I went to the bathroom. She must have gotten bored waiting on me."

Rhett sipped the cold lemonade with a nod. "Which one's yours?" he asked as he wandered closer to the table. One book was a Disney princess—Rhett wasn't up on who was who. The other looked like an adult paint book or something, with pictures of extremely detailed flowers. The Disney book had a big splotch where someone had spilled water on it. The princess' face was blue, her hair green. The other book had four red daisies amidst a dozen or so more as of yet unfinished.

"You're funny."

He shot Summer a grin.

"How's it going with Bristol?"

Rhett stopped in the act of taking a drink and lowered the glass.

"This has to be killing you."

So Summer did know he had a thing for Bristol. Probably, everyone he was around could see it. Everyone except Bristol. But Taj and his family knew for certain that Rhett wanted to be with the woman, so Summer had to know just how much this little adventure was going to cost him.

He shrugged. "Kind of."

"Look, I love Bristol, Rhett. And yes, I want her ex a million miles away from her. But I don't want to see you get hurt."

"I can handle myself, Summer," he said quietly.

"Can you, though?" She shrugged. "Because when Taj and I started seeing each other—"

"You slept with him the night you met him," Rhett reminded her with a smirk. "I'm sure it was the Santa boots and the thong."

"Actually, it was his face," she admitted, "and the thong. Anyway." She rolled her eyes at him. "We started hanging out. And we both swore we were just gonna be friends."

"I know."

"And the next thing I knew, I was in love with him." She arched her eyebrows and shook her head. "He didn't want me."

"Yes, he did," Rhett argued. "He was afraid to admit it."

"Still, Rhett, we…stopped…I mean, we didn't even break up, because we weren't together. But we stopped seeing each other. And it *hurt*."

"I know." Rhett sighed. "I know, and I appreciate your concern, Summer. But what can I do? I don't even know the whole story with her ex, but I don't want her going back to him. I don't want him anywhere near her. And I sure as hell don't want someone else cozying up to her playing her fake boyfriend."

"So, what're you gonna do about it?"

"What can I do about it?" He looked at her like she was speaking a foreign language.

"You know what I see? When I watch you two?"

"A guy so crazy about a girl he would let her walk all over him?"

Summer tipped her head, but her smile was soft and sweet. "Maybe, but Rhett, she doesn't. She would never purposely hurt you. She cares about you."

"Right." He nodded. "We're friends."

"Well, I see two people who are without a doubt meant to be together."

Rhett shook his head, but Summer held her hands up.

"Hear me out." She touched his arm. "You're friends. You care about each other. You have fun together. You spend more time together than a lot of married couples. You talk.

You *really* talk to each other. You do nice things for each other."

"Because we're friends."

"But now you have this other stuff happening. Do you know how natural you two look together? Kissing? Holding hands?" Summer stared at him with wide eyes. The back door opened again.

"Rhett. Gimme a hand out here."

"You look like soulmates," Summer whispered.

"Be right there, Taj." Rhett lifted his chin to look at his brother over Summer's shoulder. Taj leaned in through the open door, watching them.

"Want some lemonade, babe?" Summer called over her shoulder.

"Yes, please."

Rhett touched Summer's arm as he passed her, maybe to convey that even though he thought she was wrong, he appreciated her hope. Hell if he knew what to think about any of it.

"Think about it," she whispered. "Charm the hell out of her, Rhett. Make her see that she's in love with you."

twenty

. . .

RHETT

"Summer in there planning your wedding?" Taj asked when Rhett stepped outside and pulled the door closed behind him. Rhett shot a panicked look toward Stella. The last thing he needed was his niece getting excited and telling everyone he was getting married. But Stella was on her knees in the grass a few feet away, talking to Rosie. If Ellery were around, that would be cause to worry. At six, she was much more likely to pay attention to what the adults around her said.

"Nope." Rhett looked back at Taj with a grin. He knew Taj's comment was more about teasing Summer. Surely, if Taj proposed to Summer she would be a flurry of girly stuff with wedding ideas and pink stuff and confetti. But, he also knew that Taj was about to lay into him about Bristol.

And he had it coming. Because he had taken his share of potshots at Taj when he first started hanging around with Summer, insisting they were just friends. That even though they'd been hot and heavy that first night they met, it was nothing more than good friends and great sex.

"How about you?" Taj asked, head down, eyes on the far-right stake.

"Oh yeah." Rhett rolled his eyes, even though Taj wasn't looking. "I'm thinking black tux with tails."

"Nope. Tails are out."

Rhett laughed when Taj flicked his eyes up at him.

"We haven't been dating that long, man," Rhett reminded him. "No wedding bells ringing any time soon."

"Mm-hmm." Taj nodded. "You've been pining away for Bristol Miller since last November."

"You're the one with a kid on the way, living in sin with that woman in your kitchen."

Taj laughed. "Good point." He nodded and propped his hands on his hips. "But we're talking about you right now."

"What're we staring at here?" Rhett wandered closer to him and looked down at the wooden stake marking the far point of the add-on. "Watchin' grass grow?"

"Smartass." Taj dropped his hands to his sides and moseyed over to the patio where he'd left his lemonade. "Trying to decide if that's big enough. Or if we should move it out a bit more."

"You should probably ask the boss." Rhett nodded toward the kitchen as he spoke. Taj snorted and took a big drink.

"So." Taj shrugged. "Tell me. How'd this get started? I mean, what the hell, man? Summer knows about it before me?"

"The only reason Summer knew about it was because someone at the Skeleton saw Bristol and me kissing."

"Okay, even more to the point. Why didn't you tell me?"

Rhett shrugged helplessly when Taj narrowed his eyes at him. Geez, was Taj really that upset about it?

"I dunno, man. We just..." Rhett hadn't realized he was such a bad liar. "We wanted to take it slow, so neither of us told anyone. But I guess..."

"What?"

"I guess we got carried away the other night and that kiss happened, and now everyone knows."

Taj studied him for a long, quiet moment. Rhett fought the urge to squirm under his older brother's heavy stare. Did he not believe him? Was he about to call bullshit on him? Should Rhett just tell him the truth? It felt weird to have a secret with Summer. But if he came clean to Taj, then Taj would probably tell his parents. Maybe Sheridan. If they all found out he and Bristol were fake dating, then the whole thing would fall apart.

And Trey Kennedy might sweep in and romance Bristol right out of town.

Nope. He could lie to his brother.

"You guys look good together," Taj finally said. "You make it look easy."

Well, that sucked. How the hell did he make it look easy with her when she didn't see him as anything more than a friend?

"She's easy to love," he mumbled, only realizing what he'd said when he heard his voice. Taj tipped his head at him. She was, though. Rhett didn't know when it happened, exactly. When he'd gone from that attraction, the crazy crush stage, to falling in love with her. Maybe back in January. When the Skeleton Bar was dead, but he still drove there a few times a week just to see her. And they would play cards on the bar.

Sometimes they played War. Sometimes they played Slap Jack, which got crazier and more fun, if more violent, every time they played.

Maybe in February when she and Summer sponsored the Valentine's Sip Night, where they made specific cocktails and paired them with a custom playlist. Knox had installed new lighting in the bar to add more ambience or some crazy shit. Rhett listened when the girls talked, but he didn't always pay attention. He did on Valentine's, though. Bristol had worn a red dress that skimmed her little curves and hung past her knees. The turtleneck hadn't been the least bit revealing, but damned if he hadn't been hung up on the way the material hugged her breasts. She'd worn long, black heeled boots—so long, he hadn't gotten even a glimpse of her legs, but again, he'd looked his fill and fantasized even more. The lights on her long, dark waves that fell loose over her shoulders that night had made his fingers twitch with the need to touch her, run his fingers through her curls. Kiss her shiny red lips.

"She feel the same way about you?" Taj's rough voice snapped him out of his memories. Hell no, she didn't feel the same way. For all he knew, she thought of their friendship more as a sibling relationship. Then again, she probably wouldn't have laid that scorching kiss on him to start this whole charade if she thought of him that way, right?

"Isn't it too soon to know?" Rhett asked him.

"I don't know." Taj shook his head. "Like I said, you guys make it look easy."

Rhett glanced at Stella again, now flat on her back in the grass, singing a botched version of the ABC's.

"She's gonna have chigger bites."

"I know it." Taj nodded.

"When're you planning to get started on this?" Rhett waved his hand at the space Taj had marked off.

"Mmm." Taj pursed his lips. "I dunno. I would say next weekend since you're off. But we'll probably be at the ball field all weekend."

Rhett nodded. "Do it on a weeknight. We've got plenty of daylight now. I can get over here as soon as you're home from work. Hell, if we get it started together, I can show up when you're working."

"Yeah, okay." Taj walked over to Stella and nudged her sandaled foot with the toe of his work boot. "Let's go inside."

"Nope."

"I bet Summer's hungry. Let's go see."

"I want noodles."

"Okay. Let's go see what we can find." Taj leaned over and scooped Stella up from the ground. Rhett winced. Stella was tiny compared to his brother, but it bothered Rhett to see Taj move like that. He'd long-since recovered from his injuries, but his back gave him fits now and then. Maybe the stripping and dancing last winter had loosened him up. "Thanks, Rhett."

"Sure." Rhett nodded. "Don't forget Rosie." He slipped past his brother as Taj carried Stella inside. After snatching Rosie from the ground, Rhett stood for a moment. Interesting that both Summer and Taj seemed to think he and Bristol were a perfect fit. Even more so that Taj didn't know the whole thing was just a lie to hold her ex at bay until he moved on, but he still thought they made things look easy.

twenty-one

. . .

BRISTOL

The temperature, as was typical in July, was in the high 80s, but the humidity was thick enough to feel like the earth was covered with an Ugg blanket. Not terribly pleasant for outdoor activities, but Bristol loved it. The heat, the humidity, the sharp reflection of the sun off the cars in the lot—none of that bothered her. It brought back memories of her younger days. The crunch of the gravel in the parking lot under her cleats. The long, grueling hours under the sun. Long ball pants over sliding shorts and long, stirrup socks. A visor to keep the sun out of her eyes, the sweat gathering under the visor at her hairline.

Lounging on the bleachers, elbows propped at her sides, she watched Sheridan and Summer talking and elbowing each other a few rows in front of her. They were talking about wedding colors, which made Bristol ridiculously happy. Did it matter if Summer and Taj got married or simply lived together for the rest of their lives? Not a damned bit. But the idea of it—imagining Summer, beautiful in a white dress with a long train—put a smile on Bristol's face.

"Wait," she called without moving a muscle. "Did you say apricot?"

"Yeah."

"Eww. No." She shook her head.

"Not your wedding." Summer threw a batting glove at her. Bristol looked at it when it landed in her lap.

"Did I miss something? Did Taj propose?"

"No." Summer laughed as Sheridan snorted sarcastically.

"I think Summer might have to propose to him," Sheridan announced.

"Oh, come on," Summers said with another soft laugh. "Taj isn't that bad."

"Well, I'd hope you don't think so." Sheridan grinned.

"I mean, he's not kicking and screaming about never getting married again."

"But seriously?" Bristol sat up and reached for the duffel bag at her feet. "Why apricot?"

"It's pretty?" Summer shrugged.

Bristol unzipped the bag and pulled her cleats out. "Your favorite color is blue."

"It is," Summer agreed. "But I saw a dress I like, and it happened to be apricot."

"A wedding dress?" Bristol didn't look at her as she slipped her shoes on and tied them.

"No." From her tone, Bristol imagined Summer rolled her eyes.

"So, something a bridesmaid would wear. Like if I were in your wedding, I would wear an apricot dress."

"Who's getting married?"

Bristol turned as Rhett approached the bleachers. She grinned at him, her eyes roaming over him quickly. Gray sports shorts. Green uniform t-shirt. Those muscly thighs that had made her entertain dirty thoughts now and then, which made for weird beer and nacho conversations between friends.

"Summer."

"What?" Rhett whipped his head around to stare at Summer, mouth agape.

"No." Summer shook her head. "No, no, no. Sheridan and I were just talking about our favorite colors."

"Bullshit." Bristol coughed and quirked an eyebrow at her friend when she shot her a dirty look. "You're talking about bridesmaid dresses."

Rhett looked back at Bristol. "I think they should get married." He nodded.

"Me, too," Sheridan agreed. "I'd be okay with a sister-in-law. Or two."

Bristol swallowed hard when she realized Sheridan was looking at her now.

"Because," Rhett continued as if Sheridan hadn't said a word, "I want to see you in a dress again. I was thinking about that red dress you wore on Valentine's Day. You looked damn good, Bristol."

Bristol flicked her gaze from Sheridan to Rhett. Was he lying? Playing the game? Did it matter?

"Thank you," she said softly, eyes locked with his. Something about his words, the idea that he might possibly have thought she looked good before it became okay for him to say so, made her feel warm and tingly inside.

He arched his brows and leaned over to kiss her cheek.

"Why are you looking at me like that?" she whispered.

"Because I've been waiting all morning to do this."

Bristol's heart thumped so hard it hurt when he rubbed his lips over hers. Just a light touch, but she wanted him to do it again. She wanted the pressure of his warm, soft lips on hers. Not for what it looked like, but because it felt good. As if Rhett could read her mind, he kissed her again, a soft peck at the corner of her lips, and when she sighed softly, he made one more pass.

This one was the real thing. His tongue tasted like peppermint, and as she kissed him back, she thought about him brushing his teeth this morning before leaving home. Did he do that first thing in the morning? After a shower? Did he stand in front of his sink in his briefs? Or nothing at all?

That last mental image exploded in her head, and dangerous heat danced under her skin. What the hell was this about? She wasn't attracted to Rhett Bailey. Was she?

Maybe it was just that Trey had elbowed his way back into her life, and she'd loved the physical part of her relationship with him. So much so that she hadn't tried to find that same thrill with anyone else. Maybe her body was just waking up after the long slumber.

That had to be it.

She wouldn't react this way to Rhett's kiss if Trey had never come around, would she? If Trey had never come around, and she and Rhett were still just hanging out and being friends, she wouldn't be sitting here involved in a panty-melting kiss with Rhett Bailey.

"Get a room."

Apparently, Sheridan's groan brought Rhett back to reality. He broke the kiss, but he stood there by her as if claiming her as his.

"I think we should go warm up," Sheridan announced.

"If I get any warmer, you're gonna see flames shooting from my skin," Bristol mumbled.

Rhett chuckled and rubbed his hand down her back.

"Are you playing today?" Sheridan asked Summer. When Summer didn't answer immediately, Bristol forced herself to look away from Rhett. Summer was watching them.

"Yeah. I told Branch to stick me in the outfield. I'm not dumb. I know how to be careful."

"Hope Pierce shows up." Rhett stepped back from Bristol and stretched his arms over his head.

"Why wouldn't Pierce show up?" Bristol asked him.

"Bumped into him earlier at the hardware store. Some kind of shower emergency at his house."

"Great." Sheridan sighed. "What about your ex? That guy that's been hanging around?"

Bristol stared at Sheridan with big eyes. "Trey? You wanna put a glove on Trey?"

Sheridan sighed. "He's a body. And he's out there in the parking lot now talking to Knox. We're not forfeiting this game."

"Let's hope Pierce gets here." Bristol jumped off the bleachers and brushed the dust off her butt. Rhett joined in with an ornery grin. "Trey is as athletic as that rock over there."

"You two are so damned cute," Summer announced with an impish grin as she stood and climbed down the bleachers.

Bristol felt a little pinch in her belly. What the hell was going on? She and Rhett were not a couple. They weren't going to be a couple. Summer knew that. So why did it feel real when Summer said that?

twenty-two

. . .

RHETT

Rhett stepped into the batter's box and settled the bat on his shoulder. Bristol's ex was here again. Rhett wasn't sure if he was annoyed by the guy just making himself at home in Bristol's new life, annoyed that his whole circle of family and friends had welcomed the guy in, or if he should just be happy the guy was still hanging around so Rhett could capitalize on his bid to win Bristol's heart.

He swung at the first pitch and drilled the ball right back at the pitcher. If the guy hadn't moved and swung his glove up to protect himself, he would be taking a bow on the mound. As it was, Rhett trotted off the field with his bat in hand.

Summer and Taj's comments—made at different times, not when they were standing together—had given Rhett a lot to think about the past few days. Even when he'd worked the three shifts through the week to manage this weekend off for the tournament, he'd kept those comments in the back of his mind.

Cute together. Soulmates.

You make it look easy.

For fuck's sake, if anyone should know about easy, it was his older brother. Marley had put him through the ringer and broken him badly enough, Taj had sworn off love. It had taken Summer's pleasant disposition and her stubborn love and probably a lot of sexy stuff Rhett didn't want to think about to make Taj admit that he had fallen for her.

And now, Taj was happy. Taj and his little girls and Summer. And the baby they made together. Summer had given Taj a safe place to be in love. Rhett supposed after Taj stopped fighting her, she had made it easy for him.

Maybe they were seeing something between him and Bristol that Rhett couldn't see because he was too close to the situation. To the game. He wanted Bristol to want to be with him, and yet, she had never given him any indication that she felt anything other than friendship for him.

Except for the kissing.

Specifically the kiss that had happened about fifteen minutes ago. The one that had Sheridan moaning and groaning about how they needed a room. The one that made him both glad and painfully aware that he was wearing a cup, even now, two innings into the game and a streak of dirt and sweat down the side of Bristol's face.

She was in her element. God, he wished he had known her when she was in high school. Well, maybe college. She'd have been too young for him in high school. But he loved watching her play ball. Her talent, her sheer determination turned him on just as much as her sweet little ass in those damned ball pants again.

That kiss before the game had been different. For one thing, Trey couldn't have seen them. Sure, Summer and Sheridan were right there, but Bristol could have kissed him and pushed him away, citing the fact that they were in public as a reason to stop him. But she hadn't. Instead, she had kissed him back. Like she was thirsty, and he was water.

Like she needed that kiss to quench the heat inside her.

And then she'd made that comment about getting any warmer and having flames shoot out of her skin.

Was she just playing?

Rhett sighed as he crossed his arms over his chest and leaned on the fence. Tara had singled, and now Knox was up to bat. Knox had a habit of swinging for the fences, but when he toned it down, he was good.

"Glad that guy caught your line drive."

Rhett looked down at Bristol with a small grin.

"You'd have ruined his family jewels," Bristol mumbled with a shrug.

"Possibly," he agreed with a nod. "Maybe he has a wife or girlfriend who would have rubbed them for him."

Bristol snorted. "Maybe. I mean, I would for you."

Rhett dropped his head back and croaked out a laugh.

"As good as that sounds, babe," he shook his head, "I still don't wanna take a line drive off the balls."

Bristol laughed and leaned into him. Moving to settle his arm around her shoulders felt natural.

"I love watching you play ball," he told her.

"Yeah?" She looked up at him curiously. "Why?"

"Because you're so passionate about it, I guess." He shrugged. "You're a natural."

"Hmm." She nodded and peeked over his shoulder. As far as he knew, they were alone at the end of the dugout, but he wasn't sure. "Thanks."

"And I'm not saying you're the better shortstop," he quirked his eyebrow at her, "but I love looking at your ass when I'm playing left center."

"Oh my God," she laughed softly. Rhett noticed the blush flood her cheeks. "You're good at this."

"Flirting or playing along?"

Eyes locked with his, she shrugged. "I guess playing along, because it feels like you're flirting."

Both looked toward the field when they heard the clink of the bat on the ball, and everyone started yelling. Knox took off for first, but his ground ball was easily fielded by the third baseman. The double play took Tara and Knox out. Rhett smoothed his hand down Bristol's back and patted her butt.

"Three up, three down!" Pierce yelled as he trotted out of the dug out in front of Rhett. "Let's go, whiskey!"

Pierce, thankfully, had shown up two minutes before the game started. According to Bristol, they would have been better off playing a player short than putting a glove on Trey. Rhett peeked at the guy now as he trotted out to left center. Trey was sitting with his parents, nodding at something his dad was saying.

Rather than see it as a betrayal, Rhett decided it was good if his parents accepted Trey, if they liked him. That guy might get so comfortable here he would never leave. Which gave Rhett all the time in the world to make a real move on Bristol.

twenty-three

. . .

BRISTOL

They won their first game, which meant hanging out at the field and waiting to play again. Bristol had peeled her ball pants off in the cab of her truck and changed into shorts, so she wouldn't melt. The rest of the girls had done the same, though Summer had been gone for a suspiciously long time.

Bristol watched the current game from her spot under a tree a ways back from the field. Good enough to see the game and stay as cool as possible. She sipped a Gatorade and forced herself to eat a hotdog. It was too hot to eat, but then again, she couldn't play another game on an empty stomach.

Rhett was sprawled out beside her on the old quilt she'd had stashed behind the seat in her truck. On his back, he had his arms bent under his head, bare feet crossed at the ankles, and his ball cap tipped over his face. Bristol took the opportunity to look at him. Sure, he was her best friend, and she saw him all the time. But while he wasn't looking, she would help herself to some pure, unadulterated admiring.

The muscles in his upper arms were bunched tightly, his skin a shade deeper than golden brown. She skimmed her gaze over his flat belly, the spot where his t-shirt had slid up enough to reveal his skin. He was tan there, too, which made her wonder if he worked outside with his shirt off. His shorts rode up higher on his right thigh, and Bristol let her gaze linger there for a second longer.

He looked hard has a rock. His arms. His belly. His thighs.

His package.

Heat rushed her cheeks when she took in that detail. As interesting as that was, she continued her perusal and decided his calves were almost as delicious looking as his thighs. Even his feet were tan.

When she heard the low rumble of his laugh, she peeked back to find him looking at her. He'd tipped his hat back and lifted his head from the ground to watch as she checked him out.

No wonder he was hard. He was watching her look at him.

"Oh my God." She laughed softly and covered her face with her hands.

"Like what you see?"

She knew from the tone of his voice he was enjoying this. Catching her in the act. Teasing her.

"Not bad." She turned her head to look at the field. Anything but Rhett.

"Not bad?" he repeated, his voice sharp with fake outrage.

Bristol squealed as he grabbed her from behind and pulled her down to lay beside him.

"I think you liked it a bit more than not bad." He pinned her down with his hand on her chest and a thigh thrown over her legs. The weight of his palm between her breasts made it a struggle to breathe; the heat of his skin on her leg scorched her. When their eyes met, Rhett dragged his hand from her chest leaving her oddly cold and numb there. "Say it."

She grinned and shook her head.

"Say it." He sank his fingers into her hip making her jump.

"Yes, okay!" She wiggled trying to get free from under him. "Yes. Little bit better than not bad."

Rhett laughed and dropped a kiss on her cheek. Bristol closed her eyes.

Fake. This is fake. We're pretending.

Who knew Rhett would be such a good actor? He just might kill her with those soft, sweet kisses on her cheek. If he started in with forehead kisses, she might have to put a stop to this. It was one thing to kiss her on the mouth—even if they were just friends, it was sexy, but also somehow just expected of couples. But those sweet little kisses? The ones that seemed to say he cared about her?

"Careful with your wiggling," he said quietly. "I'm hard as a rock. Gonna be tenting my shorts if you keep moving."

His words took her breath away.

"You are something else," she said with a laugh. She wrapped her hand around the back of his neck and drew him close for a kiss. But instead of kissing his lips, she stole a page from his book and kissed the tip of his nose. She snatched his hat and sat up as he moved his leg to let her go. With a grin, eyes on the field again, she set the cap on her head and tugged the bill down low.

"Damn." The word sounded like a grunt. "That looks good on you."

"'Course it does." She peeked at him over her shoulder. "I'm gonna hit the little girls' room. Need anything?"

"Water?"

"You got it." She nodded as she climbed to her feet and stepped into her slides. Still wearing his hat, she felt his eyes on her as she walked away from him. She headed to the restroom still caught up in that moment with Rhett. It felt real. Dammit, this thing with Rhett felt real, and that was dangerous. She had never thought of him that way, but the way he was treating her, all charming and fun, made her consider possibilities.

Things that she wasn't ready for. Was she?

Things that could hurt if she wasn't careful.

The last thing she wanted to do was play around with Rhett—no doubt it would be fun—and then lose him as a friend.

"Hey." Summer snagged her hand as she neared the little brick building that housed the restrooms. Bristol was so lost in thought, she hadn't even seen Summer. "You okay?"

"Yeah, I'm fine." She shook her head and managed a smile for her friend.

"What's wrong? You look upset."

"I'm fine," Bristol promised. She tugged at her hand, so Summer followed her to the bathroom.

"Is it Trey? Did he say something to upset you?"

"Hmm?" Bristol ducked into a stall and stood for a moment. She squeezed her eyes closed and smacked her cheeks lightly with her fingers. "I haven't seen Trey since we played."

"Hmm." Summer's answer sounded suspiciously self-satisfied,

but Bristol was too preoccupied with the memory of Rhett holding her down and tickling her to be curious.

"Are you doing okay?" Bristol gave herself a mental shake. "Is the heat too much for you?"

"Nah. I'm okay."

It sounded like Summer was at the sink now, maybe redoing her ponytail or checking her face for sunburn. Bristol finished her business and flushed the toilet. She avoided Summer's eyes in the mirror as she washed her hands.

"Did you eat?" Summer asked when they walked back outside.

"Had a hotdog," she answered, refusing to let her mind wander to the feel of Rhett's erection pressed against her leg. That was biology, not her. He couldn't help that.

Still.

A flurry of butterfly wings swept through her stomach as she and Summer headed back toward the field.

"I'm gonna get Rhett some water. Want anything?"

"I'll come with you," Summer offered. They turned toward the parking lot and walked side by side to Rhett's truck. "Why didn't he bring the cooler up by the field?"

"Beats me." Bristol shrugged. She stood for a moment at the back of the truck.

"Bristol?"

"He's not gonna leave." She looked up at Summer. "Is he?"

"Trey?"

Bristol nodded.

"Well, he seems to be getting comfortable here."

"With my family and friends."

"What did he say to you?" Summer stepped closer to her and touched her arm.

"It's not Trey," Bristol answered. "It's Rhett."

twenty-four

. . .

RHETT

Rhett popped the top on a beer and took a big swig. Branch tossed a can to Pierce and Knox as they approached him.

"Shake Cole's up, man," Knox told Branch as he popped his open. "Asshole deserves it."

"Just because he out-hit you." Branch rolled his eyes. "And no, not shaking his beer up, because that's alcohol abuse."

They'd played and won two more games. When evening rolled around and they were done for the night, the Locklands had invited the whole team over to their place for a cookout. Rhett hadn't seen them duck out of the bleachers, but apparently, they'd left in the third or fourth inning of the last game. Harlan, the Lockland patriarch, had fired up his grill and thrown a variety of burgers, hotdogs, and brats on to cook. Jolene, like a mom to everyone, must have been in the kitchen first thing this morning to whip up potato salad, apple salad, and a garden salad.

"You two." Summer sidled up to Rhett by the cooler and bumped her hip to his. "You look like a comedy show out there."

Rhett took another long drink. The afternoon had grown hotter and more humid as the hours wore on. They'd played their second game at noon and the last at three. His Lockland t-shirt, soaked with sweat, was in the bed of his truck. He'd put on an old Kissing Springs t-shirt with the sleeves cut out before he left the ballpark.

In the second game, he and Bristol had collided in the outfield. She'd come out pretty deep for a short fly ball, and Rhett, eyes on the ball, hadn't seen her. According to their teammates, they both called each other off a couple of times and ended up smacking into each other, chest to chest, like football players celebrating a touchdown. Both had dropped the ball, but Bristol had scrambled on her knees after it, picked it up, and thrown to third where Branch put a perfect tag down on the runner as he slid.

They hadn't taken the time to laugh or celebrate on the field. Rhett had simply offered his hand to help her up and asked if she was okay. Which was a dumb question, because even if she was bleeding profusely or had a black eye in the making, she wouldn't voluntarily come off the field. Rhett wondered what kind of hellcat she had been on the field when she was younger, playing travel softball, since she was this vicious and competitive in a recreational adult league.

"Is she okay?" he asked Summer now.

He had asked after the game, and Bristol promised him she was fine. But if she wasn't, she wouldn't tell him. Not until the weekend was over, anyway.

"I think so." Summer took a drink of water and looked around the team gathered in her parents' yard. Rhett knew the moment she found Taj just from the way her lips tipped up in a sweet smile. "Did you see Trey's here?"

"I believe your mother invited him," Rhett answered with a nod.

"Rhett, my mom would invite all the other teams here for a cookout if my dad didn't put his foot down."

He laughed, but only because he knew she was right.

"Have you talked to him at all?" Summer asked him.

"Why would I do that?"

"I dunno." She shrugged. "He seems like a nice guy."

"So Bristol says," Rhett agreed. "Just kinda weird that a nice guy can't keep his dick in his pants. And stay away from younger women."

"He really hurt her."

Rhett whipped his head around to look at her. "What did she tell you?"

Summer jerked her gaze back to his and shook her head. "Nothing. Just." She shrugged and pressed her lips together. "That he cheated."

Rhett eyed her for a moment and finally looked around for Bristol. He found her standing with Marlowe and Cole, gesturing wildly with her hands. Wondering what she was talking about, Rhett had a sudden need to go stand by her.

Stand by her, hell. He wanted to go sweep her up in his arms and carry her to his truck. Get her home and give her another look at the goods he had caught her looking at earlier. Hell, maybe the back of the truck would work. He wasn't sure he could wait long enough for the drive.

As if she would want that.

Fake boyfriend, he reminded himself.

"So." Summer cleared her throat, drawing Rhett's attention away from Bristol. "Whatever you're doing, it's working."

"What?"

His dick was working, that's what. He was hard as a fucking bat right now in a crowd of family and friends. Even his parents were here. Now that wasn't going to be a pretty sight.

"Whatever you did earlier today really had her flustered." Summer patted his arm.

"Really?"

He had assumed when Bristol stood up and left him under the tree that he'd pushed it a little too far. He wondered if she was angry with him.

"Yep." Summer squeezed his arm this time. "I'm gonna go hang on your brother. Rootin' for you, man."

Rhett stood where he was for a moment, thankfully alone. He pushed Bristol, the feel of her body under his just after he had caught her checking him out, from his mind and concentrated on post-op care. Respiration. Circulation. Recording vitals. Assessing pain. Administering medications.

Satisfied that he had talked his dick down for the moment, he took another drink as he wandered over to the picnic table to grab a handful of chips.

"She's dynamite. I've never seen her play ball."

Rhett was surprised to find Trey standing beside him. Even more surprised that the guy wanted to talk to him.

"How did you never see her play ball?"

"She didn't play when she lived in Belspring. Not when we were together."

Rhett's shoulders and neck froze. Was Trey making conversation just to remind him that Bristol had once lived with him? Slept with him?

"She's..." Rhett considered his words. He was going to say awesome, but that didn't cover it. It didn't cover how smooth, how athletic she was on the field, let alone how much fun she was in everyday life. He felt Trey's eyes on him. "Everything," he finished. "She's everything."

He glanced at Trey, a little stunned at how that truth had just slipped out of his mouth. Bristol was everything, and he wanted her to be his everything. And he felt raw standing here with her ex, realizing how badly he needed to make sure she knew he wasn't playing.

Trey gave him a curt nod. "Yeah. She is."

twenty-five

• • •

BRISTOL

The crowd was still just as big in the Locklands' yard when darkness crept in around them. Bristol had nearly guzzled her first beer, but she'd slowed down and switched to water after three. No need to feel terrible tomorrow trying to play in the championship game. She was already sore from crashing into Rhett in that second game earlier today. Felt like one big bruise from her sternum down to her knees.

She ate a cheeseburger. Sat by Rhett in a circle of friends and talked about everything from a recap of the games, *Star Wars* versus *Star Trek*, and bucket list items. When Rhett finished his brat and mumbled something about still being hungry, she excused herself and filled another plate for him. Brat with mustard, just as he liked it. A serving of potato salad and a serving of apple salad. No garden salad, because he thought eating lettuce was a sin. He thanked her when she carried that and a bottle of water back to him, but he was in mid-conversation with Taj, so he was distracted.

Bristol listened to the conversation, but she found herself watching Trey. He stood several feet away talking to Pierce and Marlowe. Bristol found herself trying to figure out if he was coming onto Marlowe and then wondering why it mattered to her. The thing was, he hadn't made a play for her.

She wasn't sure if she was relieved or disappointed. Would she sleep with him? If he did make a move? No doubt she would have before.

Before she and Rhett started this pretending game. Before she saw this new side of Rhett. New to her, anyway. But really, was she doing herself any favors? Pretending to be involved with Rhett just to walk the straight and narrow and stay away from Trey? The longer this crazy game lasted with Rhett, the more likely someone would get hurt.

Then again, no matter what happened with Rhett, she knew he would always treat her with respect.

Respect. Not necessarily what she had wanted from Trey, was it? Devotion? Love? Loyalty? But if Trey had loved her, wouldn't that all translate to showing her the respect she now knew she deserved?

Head pounding, she turned with the intent to walk away. Get some air. By herself.

"Where ya goin'?" Rhett linked his fingers with hers.

"Just need some space," she mumbled. She squeezed his fingers, offered him a small smile, and stepped around his legs again. She felt someone watching her as she slipped away and knew it was Rhett. Well, Rhett and Summer.

Would she tell Summer? Later? Next week? Would she tell her about that weird moment with Rhett earlier today?

She walked quietly to the front yard, up the drive a bit. The conversations in the backyard were nonexistent out here. Arms folded over her chest, she tipped her chin up and studied the stars. Funny. She didn't know a damned thing about the constellations. But millions of stars lit up the sky, and the night sounds around her calmed her.

"Hey." Rhett was suddenly behind her. She shivered when he ran his hands from her shoulders to her elbows. "You okay?"

"Yeah." She leaned into him when he slipped his arms around her, still standing behind her.

"You sure?"

Resting on him, she closed her eyes for a moment. "Just tired. Long day."

"True." He spoke quietly, his breath warm on her ear. "But you don't seem happy."

She wasn't *unhappy*.

Uncertain how to answer him, she turned in his arms and locked eyes with him. It occurred to her that neither of them had showered after playing ball in the July humidity.

"I am." She finally shrugged.

"Not convinced." He shook his head.

Bristol rested her hands on Rhett's chest. "Tomorrow's a new day."

"What was wrong with today?"

She dragged her gaze over his face, taking in his thin lips, the dark stubble over his cheeks and his chin, his thick dark eyebrows.

"Maybe that you never kissed me?" she whispered. If he was surprised by her words, he didn't show it. Bristol's heart raced when she heard her voice. What the hell was she thinking?

"Yeah?" Rhett dipped his eyes to her mouth.

"You don't have to do this—"

This kiss was painfully intimate. Just the two of them alone in the dark on a hot summer night. His lips touched hers cautiously at first. Hungry for more, Bristol slid her hands up over his shoulders. One she cupped around the back of his neck and the other she spread over his face. He kissed her like time stood still for them, and he would take all night to taste every nuance of her lips, her tongue.

When he moved, she went with him, willingly, hand still around his neck, lips still open under his. He stroked his tongue over hers again and again; Bristol was drowning. Rhett stroked his hands down her sides to rest on her hips. Bristol felt something solid at her back and realized he had eased her up against a fence post. She broke the kiss and tipped her head back to look up at him.

"Rhett." His name was barely a breath on her lips as he ducked his head and kissed a trail down her neck. Ready to climb him, to meld her body to his—anything to put the growing fire inside her out—she moaned softly when she felt him press his thigh between her legs.

She should stop this. Push him away. Heat rushed through her again when he tugged her earlobe with his teeth. Thinking again that she should stop him, Bristol arched forward from the fence post. The move put her breasts against his chest. The pressure of his thigh between her legs zapped all thoughts of walking away.

"You okay?"

"Mmm." Eyes closed, she massaged her fingers into his neck and then up over his head, drawing a low rumble from him. Bristol felt it in his chest, pressed to hers. She wiggled just slightly on his leg, wet with the need to feel his touch.

"Let me," he whispered.

Anything. She tipped her head back on the fence post again, giving him full access to anything he wanted to do to put her fire out. Eyes locked with his, she gasped softly when Rhett tugged her right leg over his hip and slipped his fingers between her legs. The brush of his knuckles over that sensitive spot was like a match to her flame.

Rhett watched her face for a moment as he massaged her inner thigh. Lost in the heat of his skin on hers, Bristol waited, hungry, greedy, for more. When he dipped his head, she parted her lips again and met his kiss with her own. Heartbeat pounding in her throat, she moaned softly when he slipped his fingers under her shorts, her panties.

"Rhett." She shifted her hips as he stroked her core. He pressed a wet kiss to the corner of her mouth as he played between her legs. Bristol sank her fingers into his shoulders as her world tilted and spun out of control. So close, those waves of pleasure teasing and sliding away. A sob escaped her lips, desperate for release, but she wanted to draw the moment out forever. That sweet, tingly pleasure touched her toes and climbed, her nipples hard enough to hurt.

He moved his fingers around her like he was made to pleasure her. Soft and slow, teasing, and then harder and fast, until she was so close, she might go up in flames. Finally, the waves of pleasure exploded inside her, and her body tensed, the heat imploding in her core, rushing everywhere at once. Before she could make a noise, Rhett's mouth was on hers again. Bristol wanted to kiss him, but frozen with pleasure, she let him kiss her, swallow her sobs, his name on the tip of her tongue.

"I'm sorry," she whispered as she came back to her body, suddenly aware that she'd climbed her friend like a jungle gym and ridden him like a Derby horse. And come hard and fast all over his hand.

"Don't apologize." He kissed her cheek. "That was the sexiest thing I've seen in a long damned time."

She offered him a small smile when he pulled back to look her in the eyes.

"You okay?" he asked her.

Unable to find her voice, she simply nodded.

"Need a minute?"

"Please." She stroked her fingers over his lips, relieved and disappointed when he stepped away from her. Rhett stared at her a moment longer before turning to give her some space. Before he stepped away, he brushed his lips over her forehead.

Surprised, confused, Bristol watched him walk back toward the house. Her ex was out behind the house, and her friend had just delivered the hottest orgasm she had in memory just because.

And then he had gone and blown her mind.

And her heart.

With the forehead kiss.

twenty-six

• • •

RHETT

Rhett wanted to smother Bristol with attention Sunday, but he didn't. Summer might have told him to stay at it, but he thought it was best to play it cool on the ball field. Pretend he hadn't followed Bristol out to the Locklands' front yard and backed her up against a fence post to make her come. The last thing she would want right now was him being needy or placing demands on her time. Better to leave her wanting more.

At the field for the championship game, Bristol didn't exactly shy away from him. But when their eyes met the first time across the bleachers, he saw the blush in her cheeks. He imagined her face had been flushed last night for different reasons; the darkness had hidden those details from him. Now, she looked embarrassed. Rhett simply smiled, careful to keep it under a full-fledged grin. He didn't want her to think he was being cocky, that he would crow about their shared moment or that he might expect a thing in return.

Eventually, she warmed up to him, talking with him as they always did. When they took the field for the first time, Rhett on shortstop and Bristol playing left centerfield this time, they trotted out together as usual. "In Da Club" played over the little speakers hanging on the back of the rickety little concession stand, and Rhett threw down some dance moves on the dirt infield. Bristol's laugh was hearty, and when he strutted out toward her, she danced with him recklessly, a carefree smile on her face.

Rhett had no idea if Trey Kennedy was even at the field.

He didn't care.

They won the game by a run in eight innings, thanks to Taj taking one over the fence. Summer beamed from the dugout as Taj rounded the bases. Rhett took the moment to be happy for his brother. Not for the home run. While it was cool and it had been their game winning run, Taj was a big guy and had the power to do it frequently. Rhett was happy that Taj had found Summer. Even if it had started when his brother took a stripping Santa gig.

When the game was over, Rhett and Bristol walked to the parking lot together. He considered asking her if she wanted to do something, but deciding that might be pushing it, he kept his mouth shut and his ideas to himself.

"What're you doing today?" she asked him, elbows resting on his truck.

"No idea." He looked around. "Might go home and work in the yard since I'm already sweaty. You?"

"Probably laundry." She backed away, hands still resting on the truck. "And probably a giant nap."

"Did you sleep well last night?"

She froze, eyes locked with his. He wondered if they should talk about what happened. Asking if she slept well was as personal as he had been today.

"I did," she said with wide eyes. Rhett loved the little look of innocence and the nervous chuckle that followed. "Talk to you later?"

Rhett, at the back of his truck, gave her ponytail a gentle tug when she joined him there and kissed him.

"Definitely."

He watched her walk across the lot to her truck, a little bit hopeful for what might come, and a little bit let down that she didn't seem interested in talking about what they'd done. With an elbow on the truck, he waited, watched her stop and talk to Summer and Taj. Trey walked by her and gave her shoulder a squeeze. Totally innocent touch that wound Rhett up like a kid's toy, ready to smack the guy down. Worse yet, Bristol turned her head and smiled at him, said something to him—something that made him nod.

Rhett sighed and turned his back on all of them. He climbed into his truck ready to put some space between himself and Bristol. Maybe he had flustered her early yesterday. Maybe he'd gotten her off last night. But, he reminded himself, none of that meant anything. If she was still in love with her ex, if she went back to him, what could Rhett do? It would gut him, watching her throw herself back into that relationship. Fuck, it would gut him to lose her now to anyone. But to see her go back to someone who treated her so carelessly might be more than he could handle.

On the other hand, did he want to lose her as a friend, too?

He honked and waved as he pulled out of the parking lot. With some highway behind him, he turned up the radio and let Styx take his mind off the woman he had spent the last several months falling for.

The trouble, of course, was that with that kind of a head start, Bristol might never fall as fast and hard as he had.

HE HAD FINISHED CUTTING THE LAWN AND WAS JUST ABOUT finished with the trim work when his parents' car pulled into the driveway. Rhett had grown progressively surly as he worked, angry about that little exchange between Bristol and Trey in the parking lot. Angry that he would do anything for her, even pretend to be her boyfriend to keep that guy away from her, but all Trey had to do was show up and look pretty to make her swoon.

When his mom got out of the driver's seat, Rhett groaned. She was alone. And she was here on a fact-finding mission. Rhett loved his mother, but he didn't have the patience to talk to her today, to pretend to be happy about his relationship with Bristol.

He offered her a pained smile as he passed by her on his way to the garage to put the weed eater away. Her lips tipped the tiniest bit toward a smile, but she eyed him with that intense motherly curiosity that made him twitchy.

So what if he banged shit around in his garage as he hung the weed eater up on the bracket where he kept it? When he turned to look at her again, she had moved to the open doorway of the garage, but she was still watching him like she was a bad cop, sizing him up and getting ready for a beat down. Rhett almost flinched. He and his siblings had gotten a beat down a time or two when they were younger, usually from their dad, though now and then Mom had been so angry with them, she'd punished them herself. God knew, they had deserved it. Like the time they'd all been playing in the barn and Sheridan had convinced him and Taj their parents wouldn't care if they drove the John Deere around their land. Even if they were only fourteen, eleven, and eight.

Rhett wondered what his face gave away when his mom's eyebrow—just one—quirked the slightest bit.

"What?" she asked him.

"I was gonna ask you the same thing."

Rather than answer him, she continued with the stare down.

"I was thinking about the time Sheridan wrecked Dad's John Deere. In the creek."

If anything could cheer him up, it would be his mom's sweet laughter. Apparently, he was hopeless, because her laugh now did nothing for him.

"Which tells me you're feeling guilty about something."

"Am not."

Nice, Rhett. Regress to that sullen, mouthy brat.

"Let's have a beer," she suggested.

"At noon on a Sunday?"

"Rhett Charles."

Rhett sighed and led his mother into the house through the back door. He pulled two longnecks from the refrigerator, twisted the tops off them, and handed one to her.

"Spill it."

"That's alcohol abuse."

She rolled her eyes.

"What's going on with you and Bristol?"

Rhett sighed and leaned on the counter at his back. "It's complicated."

"Good thing I'm smart. Start talking."

Rhett drew in a breath so deep it puffed his chest and belly up and then held it for a moment. When he released it, he took a drink and then hung his head to study his feet. He still wore the beat-up tennis shoes he wore for yard work; they were greener with grass stains than the original white. Pieces of cut grass stuck to his sweaty legs.

"Trey Kennedy."

He didn't know what he expected his mom to say or do, but silence wasn't on the list of possibilities.

"You're jealous of her ex-boyfriend hanging around?"

He tipped his chin up and eyed her warily. As stupid as that sounded, he would go with it, so as not to give Bristol's secret away.

"Rhett, you're a catch."

"Women don't want successful catches, Mom. They want the bad boys."

"Honey." She shook her head and crossed the room to stand beside him.

"Don't hug me, Mom. I'm gross right now."

"Oh, I know." She grinned at him. "I know a lot of things. Know what else I know?"

"Bet you're gonna tell me." He drank again and ducked away when she gave him a playful swat on his arm.

"That girl loves you to the moon and back, Rhett."

Maybe.

But she wasn't *in love* with him. He wouldn't tell his mom that.

"And everyone sees it but you."

twenty-seven

. . .

BRISTOL

Bristol tasted guilt as she put her phone down on the table. This was ridiculous. Instead of running Trey off, her fake relationship with Rhett had somehow done the opposite. Trey seemed content here. More so than she'd seen him when they lived together.

"Rhett?" Trey arched his brows and glanced at her phone.

She nodded. Trey had called her—she had no idea which of her friends here had given him her number, but someone had—and asked if she would go to dinner with him one night this week. Against her better judgement, she had said yes. What harm could come from sitting down to dinner with him? They were at the Bourbon Boot Scoot with what appeared to be half of the Kissing Springs population.

She and Rhett hadn't talked—*really* talked—since the night he'd backed her up against the fence post in Harlan and Jolene Locklands' front yard and slipped his fingers inside her panties and played her like a fiddle. She was still dreaming about the tidal wave of pleasure that had started just as little splashes of sensation and then climbed her body and sent her over the edge. Well, she was dreaming about it *when she slept.*

With Trey around, with all those old memories coming up now, and with this weird thing now between her and Rhett, Bristol wasn't sleeping well. Rhett hadn't come to see her on Monday or Tuesday, and when he'd texted about getting together Wednesday night and she had told him she was doing dinner with Trey, he hadn't responded.

Until just now. While she was having dinner with Trey.

Have a nice night.

On the surface, it seemed like a nice, sincere wish. But Bristol, eyes on Trey as he talked about enjoying the rolling green and the quiet here in the Kissing Springs area, was digging deeper into Rhett's text, wondering if there was more to it.

Because it kind of sounded like a blow off. Like have a nice life. Except he very obviously didn't say *that.* Maybe she was just reading into it. Because she felt guilty. But why? Why should she feel guilty? She hadn't asked Rhett to touch her, to drive all her demons out and remind her body what it felt like to be worshipped. She hadn't asked Rhett for any of that.

But she *had* asked him to be her fake boyfriend. To protect her. Not from Trey. But from herself. And now here she was staring at the guy who broke her heart, worrying about what Rhett was doing and thinking right now.

"You look good in love," Trey said quietly.

"What?" Bristol snapped out of her thoughts and narrowed her eyes at him.

He shrugged. "You do. You guys have it. That thing—whatever it is that people have when they're in love."

"And we didn't?" she asked him. She would worry about what he actually said later. Interesting that so many people saw this big love when they looked at her and Rhett.

"No," he answered. "I never made you smile the way he does."

"We had fun."

Trey sat back in the booth and nodded, but he shifted his gaze over her shoulder. Bristol dragged her gaze down over his arm to his fingers wrapped around his glass. He had taken to drinking bourbon, though he hadn't overdone it yet. To Bristol's knowledge, he hadn't made any scenes or been falling-down drunk anywhere. Then again, Trey had never been a mean drunk; Bristol wasn't even sure he'd ever been a drunk.

His addiction went more toward women. Not even sex, though, judging from the way he used to move with her, the way he made love to her, he had been with countless numbers of women. Trey needed women to love him. He needed their attention, their affection.

Apparently, he was just too broken to return either.

"We did have fun, Bristol. But you know I wasn't gonna commit to you."

She bristled at his comment, but he held his hands up to stave off her argument.

"I'm not gonna commit to anyone," he corrected himself. "I don't know. I think I came looking for you because I was bored. Because it was time to move on. And I thought…"

"You thought that I was young enough, naïve enough, that you could find me and fuck me again and stick around just long enough to feel better about yourself and then move on."

Trey met her eyes.

"Yeah. I guess that's what I thought. And I'm a first-class ass, because I'd still love to take you back home and undress you and spend the night making love to you."

Bristol propped her elbow on the table and rested her chin in her hand.

"But tomorrow, you'd be on the move looking for someone else to love you."

He shrugged helplessly.

"I don't wanna break you and Rhett up. That looks real."

She flinched. Needing to end their dinner date, to sever this tie that Trey kept jerking from his end, Bristol cleared her throat.

"I was pregnant, Trey." Her eyes burned with tears, but damned if she would let them fall.

"What?" He sat forward and cocked his head.

"Yours." She nodded.

Unable to bear the hurt in his eyes, she snatched her phone from the table and slid out of the booth.

"Bristol—"

She hurried out the front door, Trey calling to her from the table. Outside, she walked into a wall of heat. The door of the bar closed behind her, and quiet settled around her shoulders. Those tears threatened again, but she took a moment to breathe, to calm herself.

Not ready to drive, she headed down the street on foot. He would catch up to her. And she would finish the story and then maybe…maybe Trey would pack his shit and leave the area and finally leave her alone.

And what about Rhett?

Had she blown that friendship up beyond repair? Even if Rhett wasn't angry with her for being with Trey tonight, for standing in as her fake boyfriend, would things ever be the same between them? After what happened the other night?

"Where is it?"

Not surprised to hear Trey's voice as he hurried to catch up with her, Bristol looked up as he fell into step beside her.

"What?"

"Our baby. What—? I mean—? Did you...did you—?"

Understanding suddenly that he was asking if she had aborted his child or maybe given it away, she stopped walking. Trey stopped with her and stared at her with those dark eyes, the eyes that used to make her cave to him, to love him, forgive him, nurture him.

"You were gone when I found out I was pregnant—"

"Bristol. How could you—after everything I've told you—"

"And you were gone when I miscarried," she continued, her voice small, broken. The tears spilled over her cheeks. "I didn't even know if I wanted a baby. If I was ready. But what I knew was that you were happy to be there with me, inside me, making that baby. But I wasn't enough after the first few times, and I sat alone when I did the test and waited for those pink lines to appear. And I sat alone in our bathroom, in our apartment, and miscarried your child."

Trey groaned as he took a step back from her. He lifted his hands to his face and pushed his fingertips into his eyes.

"Oh God."

"I never told anyone, Trey." She shrugged. "I was twenty-two. And I lost a baby, and you were out playing heartbroken, looking for ego strokes."

Trey scrubbed his hands over his hair and finally looked at her again with glassy eyes.

"I'm sorry."

He was. Bristol knew he was sincere. But she knew that in a day or two, he would be searching for someone to love him through this new heartache. One that didn't even belong to him.

"I know." She nodded. "I didn't tell you to make you feel guilty. I don't want to hurt you."

"Why didn't you talk to someone?"

Bristol laughed softly. "Who would I have told? My little sister?" She shook her head. "My mom? My parents knew what you were. What I was to you. They would have been so disappointed in me."

Trey pressed his lips together. Bristol broke the eye contact and dragged her gaze over his face. She watched his Adam's apple bob as he struggled with his emotions.

"Do you want me to leave?"

His question surprised her. *Did* she want him to leave?

"You seem different here." She held up a hand so as not to give him any ideas. "Not you and me. Not you and any other woman you might be sizing up. But *you* seem different. Almost content."

Trey, still struggling to accept what she had told him, dragged his hand over his head again.

"I want you to be happy, Trey," she said sincerely. "But I need you to understand I can't do that for you. I gave up trying to make you understand you have to find that inside yourself. But you need to know it's never going to happen with me. Not again."

He swallowed hard again and looked around. Maybe thinking about running again. Maybe thinking about staying. Bristol just needed him to cut the tie and walk away from her.

"You deserve better," he finally said quietly. "I'm sorry."

She caught her breath when he leaned over to kiss her cheek. So close she could smell his rich, heady cologne, the bourbon on his breath, Bristol closed her eyes. With the heat from his skin so close, she could imagine the feel of his lips on hers. The stroke of his hands on her body. The playful way he would flip her over in bed and kiss a trail down her back. The sink of his teeth in her cheeks, her thighs.

"Goodnight, Bristol."

twenty-eight

. . .

BRISTOL

When Rhett didn't show up at the Skeleton Bar again the next evening, Bristol clocked out at the end of her shift, made sure the staff was ready for a busy night as the distillery had pushed hundreds of people through for tours all day and those guests usually made their way over to the bar, and headed out to her truck without a word to anyone. Summer had waved at her as she ducked out of the gift shop, but thankfully, she was with Knox, so they were busy. Bristol didn't want to waste time chatting, not even with Summer.

Hands sweaty on the steering wheel, she rubbed them one at a time over her legs. She'd worn heels with her jeans today, and her feet hurt, but she wouldn't waste a second on stopping at her house to change clothes. Her belly rumbled with nervous energy as she pressed her foot to the gas, tearing up the asphalt, the wind in her hair. Tim McGraw's voice blared in the cab of the truck, but it didn't soothe her. Nothing would, short of seeing Rhett and figuring out what was going on. She owed him an apology, she supposed. And a fake breakup. For all she knew, he was ready for the farce to be done. Bristol had no idea if Trey would decide to settle anywhere near her, and it sure as hell wasn't Rhett's job to babysit her so she wouldn't go crawling back to her ex.

She hadn't called him, so she wasn't surprised to pull into his driveway and find the garage door closed and the house locked up. He could be inside. His truck could be in the garage, but she doubted it. With a sinking feeling in her belly, Bristol hopped out of her truck, swung her door closed, and headed to Rhett's front door. His doorbell hadn't worked since she'd met him, so she knocked hard on the door and waited with her arms crossed over her chest.

He wasn't home. Frustrated, she went back to her truck and sat for a moment, wondering what to do. Kissing Springs wasn't a big town, but it wasn't like she was going to go door to door to find him, either. She had wanted to see him, talk to him face to face, but she would have to call him now to find him. If he was trying to avoid her, a phone call would be a warning to him to stay away.

The thought sucked. She and Rhett had clicked instantly as friends, from the first time he and Taj had come into the Skeleton Bar last November. Summer had already slept with Taj and apparently, that night they decided rather than strangers doing the one-night fling, they would be friends. Bristol had seen Rhett nearly every day since then, and the fear that she had messed up that friendship because she was weak and worried she would crawl back into bed with Trey Kennedy made her sick.

She might have. If she and Rhett hadn't pretended to be dating, she might have slept with Trey again. But, she wouldn't have fallen back into that trap with him. Thinking she was special just because he pretended she was. Thinking she meant something to him, when in reality, Bristol doubted no woman meant anything more to him than another.

So, rather than messing with her friendship with Rhett, she might have gone to bed with Trey, had a few nights of incredible sex, and moved on. She might have been a little sad, a little angry with herself for caving to Trey. But she would still have that solid friendship with Rhett.

The sound of a vehicle behind her drew her gaze to the rearview mirror. Rhett. She glanced at the clock on her dashboard. Thinking about the mess she had created had taken just the few minutes necessary for Rhett to come home. Now she wouldn't have to call and sound—what? Nervous?—to talk to him. Nope. Now she had to follow him inside and apologize for being silly and look him in the eyes after he had touched her and made her come—

She gave herself a mental shake and climbed down from her truck again. Way too damned much going on in her head right now to even think about that. She didn't need to worry about Rhett and the way he had made her feel and how she wished he would do it again. Talk about blowing up a friendship.

"Hey." He glanced at her as he walked by her. "What's up?"

Bristol swallowed hard and followed him. He had opened the garage door, so she followed him inside and through the back door of the house. He wasn't dressed for work; he wouldn't work at the hospital again until next weekend. But he wasn't dressed for the work he sometimes helped his dad with—outdoor stuff, whether it be yard work or fixing gutters or fences around the pasture or even exercising the horses his parents had.

He was dressed in shorts. Khaki shorts. And a plain navy t-shirt. One that sculpted his shoulders but hung loose around his slender hips. Rhett wasn't as big, as built as Taj. But Bristol had always thought he was attractive. Now, after having her hands on his shoulders, her leg wrapped around his waist, and his thigh between her legs, she thought he was sexy as hell.

She scrubbed her hands over her face, angry with her mind for going there again.

Focus, Bristol.

Rhett was dressed like he had been out. Maybe out to eat. Or maybe out for drinks.

It was just after six, so even if it was a date, it had ended early.

Bristol swallowed a wave of jealousy. Was he seeing someone? When this was over, when they did their fake breakup, would he date someone else? Right away? Gutted at the thought, at the possibility of seeing Rhett with his arm around someone else, Rhett kissing someone else, Bristol sucked in a deep breath and leaned on his counter.

"What's going on?" he asked her.

She stared at him silently for a moment. Rhett stood in the center of the small kitchen, hands in his pockets, and watched her impatiently.

"I came here to ask you the same thing."

Rhett shook his head. "Just had dinner with Sheridan."

A sliver of relief wound its way through her, but it didn't last long. Because he didn't look happy with her, and even if he was with his sister tonight, he could and would eventually be with someone else.

"Did I do something to make you mad?" she asked, hating that her voice was so small. "Because it feels like something is wrong between us."

"Wrong beyond the fact that we did that little thing in Harlan and Jolene's yard the other night?"

She swallowed hard, nerves, fear, tingling in her fingertips.

"I didn't ask you to do that," she whispered.

"You didn't stop me, either." Rhett stepped back from her and rested his back against the front of his stove.

Stunned by his comment, Bristol wasn't sure what to say.

"I'm sorry," she mumbled finally. "It was…I didn't want you to stop."

Eyes locked across the room, Rhett shrugged. "Okay."

"Rhett." She cocked her head. "Really? We're gonna let his come between us?"

"Nope." He shrugged again, this time the movement seemed extra dramatic. "Did you sleep with him?"

"Did I—? What?"

"Did you sleep with Trey?" He spoke each word quietly, slowly, as if to make sure she heard and understood him correctly.

"No—"

"Here's what's bugging me, Bristol. No. No." He shook his head. "No. Here's the thing that *pisses* me off. The day after I touched you like that, we don't talk about it. But as I'm leaving the ball field to go home, I see your ex walk by you and touch you. And you exchange this look, and you give him a nod."

Bristol drew back, his accusation, his sharp tone, a slap in her face.

"And that means I slept with him?"

"Did you?"

"No."

"How about last night? When you blew me off. Didn't answer my texts."

"No."

"Sheridan saw you and Trey together. She said you were standing very close outside the Bourbon Boot Scoot. That—"

"Wow." She laughed softly.

"What?"

"All the way over here to talk to you, I was trying to figure out how to fake break up with you. And now, here we are, having a real argument over something that doesn't exist."

"You were going to fake break up with me?"

"I didn't sleep with him, Rhett." She threw her hands up helplessly.

"But we're still done?"

"Rhett…" She pressed her lips together and shook her head.

"We never even talked about it."

"About what we did? At Harlan and Jolene's?"

"Was it just not a big deal to you?"

She stared at him silently for a moment and finally turned to rest her elbows on the counter. "Was it a big deal for you?"

"Are you kidding me right now?" He moved forward, lunged for her, grabbing her wrist, and nearly yanking her arm off to pull her to him.

"I have no idea what you're thinking," she whispered. "I just wanna know so we can fix this."

"Maybe I don't want to fix it." He let go of her wrist and cupped his fingers around her chin. "Maybe we should just fuck it all up, Bristol."

His kiss was a little bit brutal. Their teeth clashed, her lip pinched between them. He squeezed her chin with a death grip, as if he was afraid she would disappear. It didn't hurt, though. His show of possession, his need for her, drove all thought from her head. The memory of the moment they had shared the other night alive again in her mind, in her heart, Bristol only wanted more of him.

twenty-nine

. . .

RHETT

Rhett would have stopped. He was angry, yes, but he had no intention of hurting Bristol. Forcing himself on her. But when he felt her mouth move under his, rational thought went out the window. Her fingers were gentle on his face compared to the way he held her. Lips moving with his, her tongue rubbing over his, dancing, circling his, she smoothed her fingertips over his cheekbones. The tiny mewling sounds she made in her throat made his dick throb so hard it hurt.

Easing his fingers from around her chin, he stroked both hands down her sides to cup her ass cheeks in his hands.

"No." He fought her when she lifted her legs to circle his waist.

"Please." The sob was a whisper over his parted lips. She groaned in protest again when he moved his hands from her butt to take his wallet from his pocket. Bristol backed away a step to watch him, her face a mask of anguish. Rhett lifted his eyes to hers as he pulled a condom from his wallet.

He didn't ask. She didn't answer.

Instead, she unbuttoned her jeans for him and then reached again to cup his face in her hands. Rhett tossed his wallet aside and slapped the condom down on the counter only to hook his fingers in her jeans and push them down, out of his way.

He thrilled at the feel of her hands on his shoulders, her fingers on his neck. Desperate for her body heat, Rhett cupped his hands around the backs of her thighs, groaning when his hands were full of her silky, smooth skin.

"Wait."

Her whisper was a knife in his heart. A cold fist around his cock. What if she said no? But Bristol only kicked her shoes off. The sight of her heels on his kitchen floor, the realization that she'd done it so she could get her jeans off, lit a trail of flame under his skin—to his fingertips, his thighs, his cock. He had imagined this moment with her often. Happy as fuck the time had arrived, he didn't care that it wasn't going to happen the way he had planned. No champagne. No rose petals. No romance.

After the past couple of weeks pretending with her, the kissing and the innuendo mixed with the solid love they shared as friends, Rhett was desperate to fuck her. To bury his cock balls deep inside her and feel her walls close around him. He needed her body pressed tight to him, and while he wanted his eyes and hands on every inch of her, at the moment, he didn't care that she was still half dressed. He didn't even want to take the time to look his fill at her long, slender legs or the sweet juncture of her thighs.

Later.

Rhett hoped to fuck there would be more after this, because he needed to fuck her *now*.

Bristol worked his pants open as he reached behind her for the condom. Her hands shook as she struggled with the button. The backs of her fingers were warm against his stomach, and then she slipped them under the waistband of his briefs and inched them lower. Rhett, mesmerized by the sight of her hands on his zipper, in his briefs, stood frozen with the condom still in his hand.

When she flicked her gaze up at him in askance, he moved again, hurrying to rip the foil package open and roll the condom over his thick, purple cock. They wasted no time. He dropped the foil and reached for her as she moved toward him. One hand under her ass cheek, her heat, her excitement on his fingers, he tugged her closer and drove his cock into her in one deep, desperate push. Bristol wrapped her leg around his waist and climbed him like a pole.

She was small and tight, making him worry for a moment that he would hurt her. But she nipped at his neck, his ear, and shoved a hand under his shirt collar to dig her fingernails into his back.

"Fuck me," she whispered.

Rhett carried her a few steps across the kitchen to rest her back against the refrigerator. His lips found hers for a long, wet kiss. And then he pulled out and drove into her harder and harder, sure she would cry out, that she would stop him. The months of pent-up desire for her rushed his cock, and he pounded her mercilessly against the refrigerator. Something clattered to the floor, but Rhett had eyes, hands, only for Bristol.

Eyes closed, she moved with him, thrust for thrust, and

squeezed his cock with each stroke. She sank her teeth into her lip and blinked, catching him watching her.

"Don't watch me," she whispered.

"I can't hold on." He bit the words out, angry with himself for losing control so quickly and desperate to cut loose and come inside her. "Jesus, Bristol, you're so fuckin' hot, I can't wait."

"Do it." She licked her lips as if to entice him.

He wanted to argue, insist that he needed her to come first, but Bristol slipped her hand between their bodies. One peek at her fingers sliding over her clit, her perfectly manicured red nails moving as she stroked herself, shot Rhett straight to the fucking moon.

"Fuck." He groaned.

"It's okay," she whispered, still working herself into a frenzy. "Just keep fucking me."

Her lips forming those words. Her voice begging him to fuck her. Her tight little pussy clenching his cock. And her eyes glazing as she touched herself milked his orgasm, long and hard. He wanted to watch her, to see her face as she came with his cock inside her, but he lost his battle completely and dipped his head to rest on her shoulder as the last of the shocks of pleasure rippled through him.

"Oh fuck," she sobbed as she stiffened and rode out her own orgasm. "Ohmygod. Rhett. Oh God."

"I gotcha," he whispered, caressing the spot between her ear and her shoulder with his lips. "I can stand here with you like this all fucking night, Bristol."

"I'm sorry." She laughed softly as she relaxed under him. "It's been a long time—"

"I made you come a few days ago." He lifted his head to look at her, thrilling at the serene, just-had-great-sex smile on her face.

"I know."

"Can you do it again?"

"What?"

Rhett caught her hand when she tried to pull it away from where their bodies were joined.

"Keep touching yourself. Come again."

"Really?"

"I wanna watch you this time."

"Kiss me first?"

He wouldn't make her ask twice. She leaned into him, away from the fridge, and met his open mouth with her parted lips. This kiss was slower, deeper. Rhett took the time to kiss her thoroughly, making love to her mouth, rather than the hard, desperate kissing like before.

Her fingers brushed his stomach as she moved to touch herself again. Rhett, hungry now to watch her, to see her fingers, to look at her clit as she drove herself crazy, pulled away and tipped his chin.

"Go slow."

He said it like a command, his cock twitching when she slowed her fingers in response.

"Big, lazy circles."

"Torture," she whispered. He flicked his eyes up to hers, feeling his body react again when their eyes met.

"I want—"

Bristol shook her head and rested the fingers of her free hand over his lips. "Don't talk."

"Not even to talk dirty? To tell you I wanna put my face between your legs and lick you up?"

She grinned and stroked her fingers over his lips. When her shoulders tensed, he parted his lips and nipped at her thumb. He watched her face, the way her eyes grew wide and her mouth stilled, open, as she held her breath for a second and then cut loose with a groan of pure pleasure that had him hard as steel inside her again.

"Wow." She laughed softly. "Is this how you usually do makeup sex? With real girlfriends?"

"Bristol."

She lowered her legs from his waist, her hands on his shoulders now to hold on to him. He wanted to believe she wanted more, that she wanted him to take her to his bedroom and strip her down and make love to her. But in reality, Rhett assumed she was still shaky, her body still boneless with her pleasure.

"I don't know how it could be," she mumbled, "but it's probably even better when it's not fake."

"Bristol." His voice was hard, his clipped tone enough to draw her eyes to his. "There's nothing fake about the way I feel for you."

"What?"

"Never has been."

thirty

. . .

BRISTOL

Bristol felt more naked now, after what Rhett said, than just seconds ago, when she had had her legs wound around his waist with his cock buried inside her. His words were far more intimate than the things they had just done together.

The look on his face more intense, more real, than the way he had pressed her against the refrigerator and pounded into her over and over again.

"I…" She shook her head and lowered her gaze, afraid to look him in the eyes. "I don't know what to say, Rhett."

When he didn't respond, she stepped gingerly across the kitchen and grabbed her panties form the floor where she had stripped them off minutes before.

"So. You're just gonna get dressed and walk out? Like nothing happened?"

"No." With her back to him, she stepped into the black silk, settled them low on her hips, and finally turned to look at him again. "I'm not going anywhere."

Seemingly satisfied with her answer, Rhett nodded. He pulled his briefs and shorts up, eyes on her as he zipped up.

"But I still don't know what to say."

"Tell me you didn't fuck him."

"I didn't fuck him," she whispered.

"Because Sheridan said you two looked awfully cozy." He shrugged. "And I know, it's none of my business since I'm just your fake boyfriend. But kind of sucks to have my sister telling me what she saw, asking if I'm okay, asking if—"

"I did not sleep with Trey Kennedy," she repeated. "Yes, we were…" She sighed and nudged her jeans with her toes. "We were talking. And it probably did look intimate, but nothing happened."

"What were you talking about?"

"Well." She swallowed hard and raised her eyebrows, hating that it had come to this. No matter what else was said, she would walk out of here tonight with things between her and Rhett forever changed. "I told him about his baby. That I lost. When he was with someone else."

"Bristol." Rhett flinched. "Goddammit. I wanna knock that guy's teeth down his throat."

"Well, a few minutes ago, you wanted to knock mine down my throat. Maybe you're fickle."

"I wouldn't lay a hand on you."

"I know." She shook her head. "What the hell are we doing, Rhett? I don't get anything happening right now."

"I'm in love with you," he said simply. "I have been for months."

Her belly clenched at his words; her ribs squeezing so tight, it hurt to breathe. She opened her mouth to answer him, but Rhett only shook his head.

"Don't. Don't say anything to that."

She looked at her jeans again, distracted, feeling raw, transparent, in only her panties and blouse. "I can't have this conversation like this."

"Like what? With me?"

"No." She groaned. "No, Rhett. Stop being so defensive. I just meant—"

"I can't help it, Bristol. I have lived my life entirely around you since last November. And, I know. You didn't ask me to. But, I have. Why else would I be sitting at your bar every night you work? Why would I hang around every night with you on the tailgate of your truck and talk?"

"I thought we were friends."

"We are," he agreed. "But I was attracted to you the first time I saw you, and the more I got to know you…" He shrugged. "Jesus, why else would I be your fake boyfriend? Why else would we click the way we do?"

Bristol looked away from him. Took a moment to stare out the window over his kitchen sink. Everyone she knew had pointed that out—the way she and Rhett clicked, even Trey had said so.

"Why else did I back you up against a fucking fence post and touch you like that?"

She flicked her gaze to his, still at a loss for words.

"Yeah, I get it. Some people can handle that friends-with-benefits thing. Maybe I could, too. With someone else. But

I'm in love with you, and I can't keep that to myself anymore."

Bristol nodded.

"Why didn't you tell me?" His voice was gruff.

With a sniffle, she raised her eyebrows and shook her head. "Tell you what?"

"That you lost a baby?"

"I never told anyone. Not before Trey showed up in the bar."

"And then you told him? Of all people?"

"I told Summer," she answered. Her eyes burned with the same emotion that made her throat ache. "First. And then, yes, I told Trey, because it was his baby. And even though we aren't together, even though he never even knew I was pregnant, I decided he had the right to know."

"Are you still in love with him?"

She wasn't. Even if Rhett hadn't just fucked her speechless in his kitchen in broad daylight, she would say no. Trey was right. She deserved better, and it had taken the space she'd put between them—all those miles—for her to mature enough to see that. She was just another girl to him. He was a lesson learned the hard way for her.

"No."

"I don't get what it is about him that makes you weak in the knees, Bristol. How do you still want a man who treated you so carelessly?"

"I don't, Rhett." She threw her hands out to stop him. "I don't want him. But when he first showed up here, he caught me off-guard. I haven't dated anyone since I left him. Kissing you that night in the bar was the first time I kissed anyone since I left him. I had no idea he would ever come back into my life, and I sure as hell had no idea how I would react when he did."

"So, then, now that you know yourself," he said quietly, "you were coming here to fake break up with me."

Bristol blinked, letting the tears loose.

"Actually, I wanted to apologize to you."

"For what?"

She looked around the kitchen, gaze again stopping on her jeans and her heels piled on the floor.

"Can we—can we sit down? I mean, I feel like I have ten seconds to explain myself and then you're gonna hand me my jeans and send me on my way."

Rhett squeezed his eyes closed. With an angry grunt, he stepped close enough to pull her into his arms again.

"I'm sorry." He rested his chin on her head. "I'm just… frustrated. I don't want you to just walk out on this. I know you don't love me. I don't expect you to feel that way or to say it just because. But you…we…are too good together, too important, to just throw everything away."

Bristol slipped arms around him and locked her fingers behind his back.

"I'm not going anywhere. I just don't want to do this like this. It feels like a fight, and no matter where we go from here, I don't want to fight."

"What I really want to do is take you to my bed and hold you."

Bristol tipped her head up to look at him.

"Then do that, Rhett. Because that's what I want, too."

thirty-one

. . .

RHETT

Bristol crawled into his bed like she had done so a million times before. Rhett's heart stretched his throat as she settled there on her side and waited for him to lie down beside her. Still fully clothed, he lifted his comforter and slipped into the bed. She still wore her blouse, but Rhett loved the feel of her skin on his when she scooted closer and slid her leg over his.

"I wanted to apologize," she said again. "Because I had no idea Trey would just settle in and stick around. And I…felt… guilty…for monopolizing you, your time. For asking you to pretend to be with me, because obviously, if you're doing that, you appear to be off the market."

"And?"

Head propped on her right hand, Bristol lifted her left hand to touch his lips.

"Honestly, the thought of seeing you with someone else, whether that happens tomorrow or next year, makes me sad."

"Well, it's not gonna happen," he answered simply. "Not for a long time. Because the way I love you is gonna take a long time to get over."

"And you want that?" she asked so softly he barely heard her. "To get over me?"

"No." He wrapped his hand around her wrist and kissed her fingers. "No. But I also don't want to put you on the spot and make you feel bad for not feeling the same way."

"I had no idea, Rhett," she whispered. "I mean, when I left Belspring, when I came here, dating or being in love, it was the last thing on my mind. I just needed that time to reset. To find myself again. I mean, I was twenty-two when Trey and I met. He was thirty-two. I had no idea how he would captivate me and lead me on. It took that physical break for me to see it clearly."

"I get it."

"I dated in high school. I loved my high school boyfriend with all my heart, but we went our separate ways. When I met Trey, I was this stupid, young girl who thought she knew it all. I thought I was savvy. Sexy. And really, he manipulated me and took advantage of everything I was willing to give him. I lost myself in that, in my need to rescue him."

"Rescue him from what?"

She shrugged. "Whatever trauma he sells. I bought it all."

"And the baby?"

"That was it. I was a mess when I found out I was pregnant. And then to sit alone in our apartment…and he never even knew…" She shook her head.

"Did you want the baby?"

"I don't know." She flopped back to lay on the bed and stare at his ceiling. "I don't know, Rhett. I was scared. I wasn't ready, even if I did want a baby. And as soon as I saw the pink lines—no, as soon as I was late, when I started worrying about it—I knew how messed up it was. That I was never going to change him. That I would never be enough for him. And that even if we lived together, I would be raising the baby alone."

Fingers entwined with hers now, Rhett brought her hand to his mouth and kissed it.

"But I wasn't ready to sit in our tiny little bathroom with the god-awful pea green floral wallpaper and miscarry the baby all by myself either."

"You couldn't have called someone?"

"I wouldn't call him. Because when he was out roaming, he was gone. He wasn't mine. My sister was too young to burden. My parents didn't like Trey; they were upset with me, disappointed when I moved in with him. Imagine how they would have felt if I told them I was pregnant with his baby."

"I would imagine they'd have been there for you," he said quietly. "I've met them, Bristol. They're good people."

"What Sheridan saw the other night was just me telling him. When I first said it, that I was pregnant, he thought I had an abortion." Bristol dabbed at her eyes. "Trey has some real issues with his mom. And thinking that I had aborted his baby hurt him more than me leaving him. I promised him I hadn't done that. And he told me I deserve better than him."

"He kissed you."

"Where in the hell was she?" Bristol groaned and laughed, eyes still on the ceiling. "He kissed my cheek, Rhett. He asked me if I wanted him to leave the area."

"What'd you say?"

"No. Because there's something different about him here. Not like I want him back. But he's calm here. He seems content. I don't want to be with him, Rhett, but I do want him to be happy."

Rhett sighed and ducked his head to rest on her shoulder.

"Which is why I wanted to apologize to you. To fake break up, because it's not fair for me to drag you along on this self-preservation game if Trey's going to stick around."

"If we fake break up and you sleep with him, even if it's just once, it'll kill me, Bristol."

"Why didn't you tell me?" she whispered. When Rhett didn't answer her, she smoothed her hand over his face and kissed his cheek. "Why didn't you tell me how you felt?"

"Because you made it clear you weren't interested in dating anyone."

"So you gave up?"

"I was biding my time." He lifted his head and gave her a lazy grin. "Hoping to find the right time to sweep you off your feet."

"You did it," she told him. "You did, Rhett, but I'm still catching up."

"That night? At Harlan and—"

"No." She shook her head. "That morning. When you pushed me down on the blanket under the tree. I wanted you so much right then. I wanted the world to go away, so it was just me and you."

"You don't have to say that."

"I'm just scared, Rhett."

"Of what?"

"Losing you."

"We had a fight, Bristol. It happens."

"Yeah, but how many friends fuck like we just did and have a fight and save everything?"

"Doesn't matter, because we're talking about us."

Bristol lifted her head from the pillow to kiss him.

"I want to do it again." She drew back to look at him. "But this time, I want to be naked with you. Right here."

"Are you sure?"

"It's the one thing I am so damned sure of right now."

Rhett sat up to shuck his shirt and shorts off. But he stopped her when she reached for the buttons of her blouse.

"What?" She stared at his hand on her arm.

"Let me?" he asked softly. "Let me undress you. I've thought about this moment for so long, Bristol. I wanna take your panties off with my teeth and taste you."

Bristol dropped her arms back to the bed, above her head and offered him a slow, sexy smile.

"I like the sound of that."

thirty-two

. . .

BRISTOL

Fingers in his hair, Bristol writhed under Rhett as he played between her legs. The frantic, hard sex in the kitchen had been delicious. Bristol hadn't been a virgin when she started seeing Trey, but she wasn't terribly experienced, either. Trey had played her body like an instrument, always knowing where to touch her, how to touch her, to drive her out of her mind. It was Trey who sweet and dirty talked her, who made her relax and understand what her body was telling her, what she wanted and needed.

But with Rhett, it was better. She hadn't known the first time he fucked her how he felt about her. But still, their friendship was stronger than her relationship with Trey ever was. That bond made that first time intense in a way that was new to her. Now, though, Rhett had done what he said he wanted to. Naked, his proud cock thick and hard for her, he had eased a knee between her legs and unbuttoned her blouse painstakingly slowly. Bristol had fought the need to urge him on, to hurry. To shove her desperation out of her mind, she concentrated on his face as he undressed her. The lust in his eyes when he parted her blouse to reveal her black silk bra.

She had moved for him, sat up so he could push her blouse over her shoulders and then her bra straps, too. He tossed her blouse aside and then took the time to bury his face between her breasts and stroke her curves through the silk. His gentle pinches over her nipples had drawn a whimper of need from her, but she had waited, letting him have control.

When, finally, he unhooked her bra and pulled it from her, her nipples were hard little beads awaiting his touch. His mouth. Rhett didn't disappoint her. Rather, he gathered her breast in his hand and squeezed firmly, pushing her nipple out in invitation. Bristol had hummed her appreciation, her pleasure, when he closed his lips around her and suckled her into his mouth. With his other hand, he stroked her other breast, rolling her nipple with his thumb.

Wild with need to feel his touch, his tongue, between her legs, Bristol had lifted her hips from the bed to grind against his cock. Understanding her demand, Rhett had released her nipple and dragged his open mouth down over her belly until he caught the elastic of her panties in his teeth. So ready for his promise, Bristol had quivered with anticipation just at the feel of the silk sliding from her hips, over her mound and thighs.

And now, his face buried between her spread legs, Rhett kissed her in the most intimate way. Bristol's whole body was in flames, the center of the fire in the core of her body. Rhett scissored his fingers inside her while he pummeled her clit with his tongue and his teeth. He hadn't stopped even when she'd come hard just a few seconds later. He only lifted his head for a moment to grin at her, lick his lips, and go back for more.

Gone were the worries about hurting him. About getting hurt. The future of their friendship. The wonder of Rhett admitting his feelings for her. Everything in her world at the moment was the way Rhett flattened his tongue over her clit and then flicked it over and over again with the tip of his tongue. The sting of his teeth. The slide of his fingers over the spot he'd found inside her that made her quiver.

Bristol felt the pleasure and pain building again, so high, so hard, it scared her. And still, Rhett pushed her, sucking her clit into his mouth. She shattered, hands sliding away from him, flopping on the bed, as he lapped at her.

"Your wallet's in the other room," she whispered. "I can't wait that long for you to be inside me."

"You are the sexiest woman I have ever seen."

Bristol opened her eyes as he stretched and leaned over her to reach a drawer in his nightstand. She turned her head and watched him take a box of condoms from it.

"Oh, thank God."

Rhett tore the foil package open and rolled the rubber over his cock.

"Are you sore? From before?"

"No."

"You will be," he reminded her.

"Worth it," she answered.

He caught her hand when she reached to touch his cock.

"Do that now, and it's gonna be a little longer before I can bury myself in that sweet, little pussy."

"Oh my God." She grinned. "Rhett Bailey is talking dirty to me."

"You know how many nights I've fantasized about taking you on the bar at the Skeleton?"

"Tell me."

"I think sprinkling a little bourbon right here," he stroked his fingers down her seam and quirked an eyebrow at her, "And then licking it all up would put Lockland over the top of the market."

"That spot's just for you." She shook her head.

"If you keep talkin' like that, I'm gonna come before we get started."

"Then get started." She lifted her hips again. "Please."

Rhett shifted his weight as she settled her hands on his hips to guide him in. He poked at her, eased the tip of his cock into her folds. Eyes locked with hers, he stopped for a moment.

"Still okay?"

"No. I need more."

"You're so fuckin' tight, Bristol. You're a wet dream."

She didn't do it to spur him on, but because she ached to feel him inside her. Her body was spread out before him, ready to take him in, and ready to fly apart at his touch again. Rhett's eyes popped when she cupped her breasts in her hands and squeezed her nipples between her fingers.

He pushed harder, further a bit at a time, until he stretched her to accommodate him.

"I love you," he told her again as he moved inside her. Bristol, too afraid, too distracted, too full of him, met his parted lips with her own and let any words she might have said in return get swallowed up in the kiss.

Slow, passionate lovemaking with Rhett Bailey was even better than the crazy, frenzied sex in the kitchen.

When it was over, Rhett lay on his back, Bristol with her head on his chest. Satiated, tired, and content to be with him this way, Bristol closed her eyes and considered everything that had happened lately. Trey Kennedy showing up at the Skeleton Bar was the last damned thing she had wanted or needed, and yet, Trey's reappearance in her life had led her right to Rhett. To this moment.

Rhett loved her.

"Does anyone know?" she whispered. "About us? That maybe it's real?"

"Everyone knows, Bristol," he answered. "Everyone but you."

thirty-three

• • •

BRISTOL

Sheridan eyed her coolly as she sat down across the table from her. French Kiss Coffee was busy again this morning. Bristol sipped her latte as Rhett's sister put her cup of plain black coffee on the table, rested her elbow near it, and plopped her chin in her hand. Now that she was face to face with Sheridan, Bristol couldn't help but think she should have ordered black coffee. She needed something strong to do this. Maybe even a shot of bourbon in black coffee would have been a good idea.

As much as she liked Sheridan, Bristol would rather be sitting here with Summer. Sharing some details, though not all, and crooning about good sex, and maybe dissecting every damned thing that had happened since Trey showed up, hoping to understand what she was feeling.

Not sitting here with Rhett's sister who was angry with her. As far as Sheridan knew, Bristol was cheating on Rhett.

"So?"

Bristol leaned forward to rest her elbows on the table, too. But rather than speak, she ducked her head and dragged her fingers back through her long, loose curls.

"It's not what you think," she finally mumbled.

"Of course it's not." Sheridan rolled her eyes and sat up straight. "Is that what this is about? We're gonna sit here, and you're gonna deny cheating on my brother? And you think we're going to just—what? Pretend that's okay? I've been gone for a while, Bristol, but I know my brother. I know he's crazy about—"

"Can I talk?" Bristol interrupted her quietly. "I like you. I like your parents and Taj. I especially like Rhett, and the last thing I would ever do is hurt him."

Sheridan sighed and shrugged, ready to listen but obviously unconvinced that Bristol was being honest.

"Rhett and I aren't dating."

"What?"

"We were never dating."

"What do you call it, Bristol? When you hang all over each other and steal kisses and look like you're in love in front of the whole damned world?"

Bristol hesitated. *What were she and Rhett doing?* Fake dating, yes, but was that over now? Were they seeing each other? The hell if she knew. She loved him, yes, but she wasn't ready to say she was *in love* with him. That would look like she was just jumping on board with him because she felt obligated to say it, and it might end up hurting them both again in the long run.

"Rhett and I have been friends since last year. When Taj and Summer hooked up."

"I know." Sheridan nodded, obviously still not impressed.

"When Trey Kennedy showed up at the bar when I was working, I panicked. And told Trey I had plans with Rhett. That we were together. And then I kissed Rhett in front of Trey. To make it believable."

"So that's the kiss everyone was buzzing about a while back."

Bristol nodded.

"You know why it was believable? Because my brother is in love with you."

"Sheridan, I didn't use him," Bristol argued. "Well, I did, but we talked about it. And he was on board. We were going to pretend to be together until Trey left town."

"Great." Sheridan nodded.

"I don't want to hurt Rhett."

"Bristol, you already have. Asking him to pose as your boyfriend. He would lay down and do anything for you, let you walk all over him. Because—"

"We talked," Bristol cut her off again. "Look, Rhett and I talked last week. After you told him you saw me with Trey. Okay? Things are really complicated, but I promise you, there are no secrets between me and Rhett."

Sheridan took a drink of her coffee and left her fingers on the cup when she put it back down. "What does that even mean?"

"You asked me if we were sleeping together."

Sheridan nodded.

"Well. We are now."

"To keep it believable?"

"No," Bristol insisted.

"Look, whatever game it is you're playing, whether Rhett says he's in or not, you're gonna hurt him. Everyone in Kissing Springs can look at the two of you and see how much he loves you. Everyone but you. How long will you make him work for it? How long before you dump him?"

Bristol heard Gary, the owner of French Kiss, talking to someone at the counter. She glanced over her shoulder wishing she could slip away and talk to him, or just run like hell from Rhett's sister.

"I can't answer you, Sheridan. Because I don't know what's going on with us. But I am not hiding anything from Rhett."

"'kay." Sheridan nodded. "Well, please understand that until you and Rhett get this figured out, I can't be fun and friendly with you. I watched Taj's ex-wife stick a knife in his back and drive it deeper every day. I can't do that again. Either you're in love with Rhett, or you're not."

Stunned by Sheridan's cool delivery, by the harsh words themselves, Bristol sat frozen, as Sheridan picked up her cup and stood. She walked away from the table without a second glance; Bristol looked back over her shoulder to see Sheridan put her nearly full cup in a bussing container on a trash can by the door and walk out.

She understood Sheridan's position. She loved that Sheridan had Rhett's back. But that didn't make what Bristol felt any easier to understand.

Either you're in love with Rhett, or you're not.

Was it that simple?

She flipped her phone over and looked at the screen. The sting of Sheridan's attack still under her skin, Bristol didn't want to talk to Summer. What if she felt the same way? Summer had known how Rhett felt about her and kept it from her. What if she was angry at Bristol for not seeing through Rhett's friendship ploy?

"This seat taken?"

Bristol tipped her head back and found herself staring at Rhett's mom. She laughed softly and shook her head.

"No, but you don't need to read me the riot act. Sheridan just did."

"Saw her outside," Claire said with a nod. She pulled Sheridan's chair out a bit and perched on the edge. "I'm sorry. She's very protective of her brothers. Especially after the number Marley did on Taj."

Bristol nodded. "I get that. I don't know how to say I don't want to hurt him any other way than saying I don't want to hurt him."

"But?"

"I'm scared, Claire. This is new to me. I mean…Rhett's been feeling this way for months, and I…I thought we were friends. I thought that bond between us was friendship."

"Mind if I grab some coffee? Will you wait?"

Bristol nodded and waved Claire over to the counter. She had no desire to sit with Rhett's mom for another lecture on how she was treating him, but she certainly wouldn't just slip out and ditch her when Claire's back was turned, either. She fiddled with her phone, but she didn't text anyone. No way she was ready to talk to her mom about any of this. And she didn't want to burden her little sister.

Claire was back a moment later with a cup of black coffee, same as Sheridan's.

"I'm sorry."

Bristol frowned and shook her head. "Why are you sorry?"

"I was worried Rhett would rush into this once you started dating."

"Oh." Bristol sucked in a deep breath and let it out slowly.

"Sweetheart, he's been talking about you for months."

Bristol swallowed hard.

"I know you've been good friends. I just don't want him to scare you away with all those big feelings he has for you."

Bristol nibbled on her lip while she considered Claire's comments. She wasn't afraid of Rhett. She wasn't afraid of being with him, obviously. Even after the shotgun sex in his kitchen, after he confessed to being in love with her, Bristol had climbed into his bed with him. She had wanted him to make love to her, and when it was over, she wanted to stay there in his arms.

She wasn't afraid of Rhett. Or his feelings.

She was afraid of what would come next. Sure, they might work out and be happy—whether that meant dating or living together or marriage somewhere down the line. But they might burn hot and bright for a few months and then burn out and find they couldn't stand each other.

What then?

"It's a lot," she whispered finally. "It's a lot to process."

"You lived with Trey?" Claire sipped her coffee.

"Yeah." Bristol's quiet laugh was humorless. "I did."

"I know he hurt you." Claire reached over the table to touch Bristol's hand. "But I raised my son to know how to be in love with one woman. He's not going to hurt you, Bristol. Not like that."

thirty-four

• • •

RHETT

"What the hell?" Taj twisted the top off a beer and stared at Rhett with the frown that used to make him nervous. When they were kids, Taj could and did knock him on his ass a time or two. Their mom wasn't stupid; she always seemed to know who started every fight. She wasn't weak, either. No matter who started it, Claire Bailey ended it.

Now, though, Rhett wasn't scared of Taj. More like annoyed with him. And even more annoyed with Sheridan.

"Thanks." He turned to his sister with an eye roll.

"You're not dating?" Taj repeated. "Seriously?"

Rhett groaned and waved his hand at the new concrete slab on the back of Summer and Taj's house. Ellery and Stella had dragged him outside the other night to show him their handprints in the cement. All four of them in a neat row—Taj's, Summer's, Ellery's, and Stella's. A nice little family. It had made Rhett think of the stick figure families plastered on the back window of damned near every mini van in the area.

Funny how it made him bristle with disdain and jealous as hell of his brother. He wanted that and more with Bristol Miller.

"Why couldn't you just stay out of this?" he asked Sheridan. "I came over here to see if Taj wanted some help with framing the walls for the addition, and instead, I gotta stand here and listen to this bullshit."

"I just don't think she's good enough for you," Sheridan said with a shrug. "If that's all she wants from you. If that's how she's going to treat you."

"Okay." Rhett shook his head and held up a hand to stop his sister. "First? I am an adult. Second? I'm not stupid, Sher. I knew from the second she told that guy she and I had plans that I would do whatever I needed to do to protect her from him."

"Because, what? Is he gonna sneak into her house and attack her?"

"Because he's ten years older than she is, and he groomed her when they met in Belspring, and he manipulated her into staying in a relationship."

"Trey's not a *bad* guy," Sheridan said quietly. "He's just a cocky jerk who's a little too proud of his—"

"Bristol is still Bristol," Rhett cut her off. "She's still the fun, charismatic bartender at the Skeleton Bar. She still plays a killer shortstop in league ball. She still loves hanging out with you and Summer. She loves Ellery and Stella."

Sheridan and Taj stared at him silently.

"She was twenty-two when she started seeing him. Do you remember being twenty-two, Sheridan? If a guy like Trey had come along and swept you off your feet, you'd have fallen under his spell the same fucking way she did."

"But she left him," Sheridan reminded him. Taj took another long pull from his beer.

"She did." Rhett nodded. "But I think we've all probably gone back to an ex for sex and then regretted it. I have."

Sheridan's sigh was long and loud, as if she was put out by having to admit the same.

"He's got the bad boy vibe, Sher. For some reason, women swoon for that shit."

"Not all women," she corrected him.

"I will admit that when she kissed me that first night, it took me by surprise. But when we talked about it later, when she said she was afraid she wasn't strong enough to stay away from him, I told her I was happy to be her fake boyfriend. Just until he was gone."

Sheridan shrugged and shook her head. "So, does this guy have like a bionic dick or something? Is he so incredible in bed that she can't trust herself to stay away from him?"

"Harsh." Taj tssked, eyes on their sister.

"Have a heart, Sheridan," Rhett said quietly. "You liked her until you found—"

"I do like her," Sheridan mumbled. "But after watching Marley tear Taj up, the last damned thing I want to see is someone doing that to you."

"I can take care of myself," Rhett promised her. "And this is a totally different situation."

"Where's Summer?" Sheridan glanced at Taj.

"She's with Knox. They're looking to break ground on their amphitheater in the next month or so. Planning meeting or something."

"Does she know?"

Rhett stared at Sheridan wondering why she couldn't just keep her mouth shut.

"Yes," he said without looking at Taj. "Thank you for putting me on the spot again. Now Taj is gonna be pissed at Summer."

"Nope." Taj shook his head. "Look, Sher, I get it. I don't wanna see Rhett get hurt, either. But I've been around Bristol just as much as you have. She's not out to hurt anyone, especially not Rhett."

Sheridan folded her arms over her chest.

"And, as someone who's been on that side of that kind of hurt, I get that Bristol talked to Summer. She needed someone to listen."

"Okay." Sheridan nodded. "Fine. I'll keep my mouth shut and reserve judgment. But if she—"

"We need to find her a guy." Rhett pointed at Sheridan and looked at Taj. "She needs someone to keep her busy so she'll stay out of my business."

Sheridan snorted. "I do not need a guy. That's for damned sure."

"See, there's a story there," Taj agreed with Rhett. "Why you came back home. Alone."

"Because I needed a change of scenery," she answered simply. "I don't need a guy. Maybe a job."

"You have a job."

"Yeah, working at the grocery store for just above minimum wage isn't for me. I need to figure something out or change the scenery again."

"Where would you go?" Taj asked her.

"No idea. But Kissing Springs has a few hair salons. One more might be too many cooks in the kitchen."

"So do dog grooming," Rhett suggested. "Anything. Please just lay off Bristol? She likes you, Sheridan."

"Did you just suggest I should be a dog groomer?"

"Posh doggie salon in Kissing Springs." Rhett tipped his head. "I can see it."

"Lots of couples put their dogs in their weddings now," Taj agreed. "You could offer wedding day grooming."

"I think you guys started early," Sheridan answered as she drained her beer. "And you're drunk already."

"Where're you going?" Taj asked as she opened the back door of the house. "We're just getting started here."

"Mom and I are going out for dinner."

"Great." Rhett nodded. "Please refrain from discussing me and Bristol with mom."

"Goodbye Bailey boys," Sheridan called as she stepped inside and closed the door.

"Next time she comes over, I'll make sure the girls are here," Taj announced as he drained his beer. "They'll keep her busy, so you don't have to go through more of that."

"You're on my side? Really?"

Taj shrugged. "I like Bristol. And while I get along fine with Trey Kennedy, it's fucking weird that he followed her here after such a long time. I want her to be happy. Whatever that looks like for her."

Rhett nodded. "Thanks."

thirty-five

. . .

BRISTOL

Bristol felt Rhett's eyes on her as she licked her ice cream cone. His attention, now that she knew what he was thinking and feeling each time she caught him looking at her, made her blush. Even after the night that wild, crazy desire between them exploded in his kitchen, Rhett Bailey could still make her blush.

"What?" she asked without looking at him.

"You."

He did that a lot, too. Said silly little sweet things that made her belly feel twitchy and nervous. She peeked at him on the other end of the park bench. His intense stare lit a fire in her belly. They hadn't made love again. Not since that first night.

Rhett had announced that he would either back off and stay friends, or he wanted to court her. Date her. Romance her. But he had put the ball in her court. Over the bar, when she was at work, he had talked in that low, sexy voice about how making love to her that night had completed him. That every day with her was a gift, and that being with her that way was priceless. And then he'd made his promise and told her it was up to her. He loved her too much to pressure her.

Frazzled, Bristol had made an Old-Fashioned that went horribly wrong, dropped a rocks glass and cut herself cleaning it up, and finally offered him a small smile. She asked him for time. Rhett, being the laid back, kindhearted man he was, had simply nodded. Mess on the floor cleaned up, a bandage on her hand, and a remade Old-Fashioned and apology to her customer later, Bristol had come back to stand opposite the bar from him.

"Maybe we could go to a Louisville Bats game."

Rhett's grin lit up the bar. "Are you asking me on a date, Bristol Miller?"

"I think I am," she had whispered.

They hadn't made it to a game yet. But they had gone out a few times. Pizza at The Black Olive. Dancing at the Bourbon Boot Scoot—so far, Bristol's favorite date. Moving to the beat of the music, all the while in Rhett's arms. They had strolled the square in Kissing Springs on late summer nights like this one.

"It's interesting that you like butter pecan ice cream."

"Why?" She tipped her head at him as she crunched into her cone.

"Because I like chocolate," he answered. "And then when we kiss, it's a nice mix."

"Wow." She laughed and shook her head. "That's a stretch."

Rhett, each time they went out, had taken to arguing that they were soulmates. Bristol tended to agree with him, with each day that passed. But not because of his goofy arguments.

Butter pecan and chocolate kisses, for Pete's sake. His argument the other day that he hated green beans, but she ate them when they went for dinner at Two Fourteen. Bristol had corrected him—haricot vert—and said that didn't make them soulmates. His next argument was that she liked peach pie, and he liked apple—both fruits, so that meant something.

Bristol had agreed; it meant that he was crazy.

He had slipped then, and said yes, he was, crazy in love.

He tried the argument that she was a bartender and he liked beer. She had only rolled her eyes at him.

They were soulmates. She had no doubts anymore. But the proof for her was in the way she finished his sentences for him. The way he read her mind when she needed something—whether it was a snack or a hug. Watching movies with him. Laughing with him on the ball field, doing that ridiculous dance thing he'd made up for "In Da Club." Watching with her heart in her throat when he rushed to first base, struck the bag so hard he popped an ankle and went down. Sitting with him in the clinic for the x-ray. Laughing in relief when they found it was just a sprain.

Going to bed alone at night, irritated that she had to stop and sleep, because all she wanted was to be with Rhett Bailey.

"You know what's funny?" he asked as she finished her cone.

"What's funny?"

"Let's walk." He stood and reached for her hand. Bristol twined her fingers with his and looked up at him as they walked down the sidewalk. "Ellery found Taj's bag last year. His Santa bag."

Bristol snorted softly. "The suit he wore when he was stripping?"

"That one." Rhett nodded. "She asked him the other day if he was going to be Santa's helper again this Christmas."

"Oh boy." Bristol grinned. "Hey, wait'll Taj and Summer's baby is older, and he or she finds out how Taj and Summer met."

"Have you ever gone?" Rhett nodded toward the Boyd Theater across the street. "To the show?"

"Yep."

"Really?"

"Yeah. One of my friends from college came down last winter. We went together. And then went out drinking."

"Did you like it? The show?"

"Well, I mean, a bunch of hot guys stripping down and dancing? What's not to like, Rhett?"

"Taj wasn't part of that, was he?"

Bristol laughed softly. "Are you worried that I've seen your brother's package?"

"Well," Rhett shrugged. "He keeps that part covered."

"Oh, I know." She nodded.

"How do you know?" Rhett yelped. "Seriously?"

"Because Summer told me all about how hot his ass was in the little red Santa thong." Bristol squeezed his fingers and leaned into him. "I have never seen your brother anywhere near naked. And I won't. He's not doing that anymore, remember?"

"I'm still a little shell-shocked that he ever did it."

"Imagine being your mom."

"Wait." Rhett tipped his head with a frown. "What?"

"Well, she saw the show. For one of her friend's retirement parties or something."

"My mom saw—?"

"Taj wasn't there," Bristol reassured him. "It's okay, Rhett. Breathe."

"But." He swallowed hard and pounded his fist into his chest like he had heartburn. "Mom? Was at a party with strippers?"

"Mmm." Bristol nodded. "Maybe we should change the subject."

"We most definitely should," he agreed.

"Good. Because there's something I've been meaning to tell you."

She stopped walking in front of the Lock Bridge, but she faced Rhett.

"Well, now I'm scared."

"I love you, Rhett." Her voice was no more than a hoarse whisper. "I've loved you all this time and didn't even know it."

"Then how do you know it now?"

"I've never felt this way before," she said quietly. "Everything with you, everything you and I have ever done together, makes me happy. And when we say goodbye at the end of every night, I go to bed counting the hours until I get to see you again."

When Rhett cupped her face in his hands, Bristol covered them with her own.

"If that doesn't make us soulmates, I don't know what does, Rhett Bailey."

epilogue

. . .

RHETT

Rhett stood with Taj, both leaning on the metal fencing around the dig. Summer and Knox, both in yellow construction hats and work boots, stood behind the fence with the guy running the backhoe. Lockland Distilling had officially broken ground on the amphitheater earlier today. Right now, Rhett thought it looked like a giant playground. Dirt. Little bit of mud. And excavating equipment. The only thing missing might be whiskey, but they could turn around and walk back up through the parking lot to the Skeleton Bar for a pour if they wanted.

Bristol was working. She would pour them both a little something for free. And then knowing Bristol as he did, Rhett knew she would throw cash in from her pocket to cover it.

They were going out later—the five of them: Rhett and Bristol, Taj and Summer, and Knox. Rhett hadn't been around Knox much, other than their softball games. Sounded like he and Summer clashed quite a bit when she had first moved home. In fact, Taj had jokingly said something about setting Sheridan up with him and Summer had come unglued and smacked Taj on the back of the head.

It would be nice, though, Rhett thought as he and Taj watched Knox and Summer talking to Max Konrath—the foreman on the excavating team. The backhoe driver leaned over to listen, too. Their voices carried just enough for Rhett to hear them, but not enough to make out what they discussed.

Sheridan had warmed to Bristol a bit. They had gone out for lunch after that coffee mishap at French Kiss. Rhett had considered yanking Sheridan's braid off her head when he found out about that. But Sheridan was still a little cool with Bristol, and though she claimed to understand, Bristol was a little gun shy around Sheridan now.

Not the dynamic Rhett wanted. Not when he fully intended to have Bristol in his life forever.

"Kinda hot, isn't it?" Taj asked in a low, rumbling voice.

It was warm, but Rhett didn't think it was too bad. And he was wearing jeans, same as Taj. He shrugged, eyes still on the mess beyond the fencing.

"I don't know what that woman could wear that wouldn't turn me on," Taj mumbled.

"Oh." Rhett nodded as realization dawned on him. Taj meant Summer was hot. In the construction hat and boots.

"She climbed the ladder to my loft in—"

Rhett shook his head. "Bristol and I knocked magnets off my refrigerator." He locked eyes with Taj. "Let's not do this."

Taj laughed and nodded.

"We're lucky sons-of-bitches, Rhett."

"That we are," Rhett agreed.

"Hey." Summer flashed them a smile as she and Knox walked the turned-up ground toward them. "Lemme just change my shoes."

"I kinda like 'em." Taj's comment drew an eye roll from Rhett.

"You would." She laughed softly. "Is Bristol ready?"

"She said to give her a few more minutes."

"This baby is hungry." Summer rubbed her little belly as she headed toward the main building. "Be right back."

"You hoping for a boy?" Rhett asked Taj. Knox followed Summer into the main building.

"Nah." Taj shook his head. "Imagine what kind of beautiful little girl I could have with Summer. Imagine three little beauties."

"Yeah." Rhett nodded. "Imagine."

Taj met his eyes and laughed, even as he mumbled a string of swear words strong enough to curdle milk.

"Right?" Rhett said. "Imagine being the father of three beautiful daughters. Ellery and Stella need a brother to protect them."

"Didn't you just give Sheridan hell about getting in your business?" Taj asked as they walked toward the parking lot.

"That's different."

The door of the bar opened, and Bristol strolled out in jeans, heels, and a crisp-white blouse. Her hair hung in long, loose curls down her back.

"Where is Sheridan tonight?" Rhett asked Taj.

"Some friend from Scottsdale is visiting. I'm sure they're out raising hell."

"Hey!" Bristol threw her arms around Rhett's shoulders and kissed him. "How was your day?"

"Good and better now."

"Summer coming?" She leaned around Rhett to look at Taj.

"Yeah. She went to change her shoes."

"Hmm." Bristol arched her eyebrows thoughtfully. "In her office?"

"Yeah."

"Hmm." She looked at Taj again. "She might need help."

Taj's rumble of laughter made Rhett turn to look at him.

"Knox is in the building. I don't think so."

"Knox is right there." Bristol nodded her head at Knox as he headed to the parking lot.

"Hey!" Knox called. "Gotta run by the house and grab a few things. Meet ya at Two Fourteen."

"Hmm."

"Mmm-hmm." Taj nodded.

"What the hell is going on with you two?" Rhett snapped.

"Summer needs my help," Taj told him.

"With what?"

"She can't lean over to tie her shoes anymore."

"She's hardly even showing yet."

"Rhett." Bristol drew away, stroked her fingers down his arm, and took him by the hand. "I need help."

"With what?" He swung his gaze back to her, nearly tripping over his own feet when he saw the look on her face. "Here?"

"Mmm-hmm." She nodded.

"On the bar?"

"You wish!" She dropped her head back with a laugh. "No. Not on the bar. In my office."

"Can we use the bourbon?"

"What if you spill some on my jeans?"

"I promise I'll lick up every last drop."

THE END

KEEP READING FOR CHAPTER 1 OF BOURBON & BEDPOSTS.

bourbon & bedposts

The asshat with the jackhammer could stop anytime. Good grief. There should be a law against that bullshit. Who the hell was making so much noise on a Sunday morning?

Sheridan Bailey cracked her eyes open slightly and grunted at the flash of pain. The room spun a bit, making her dizzy like when she and her brothers rode the county fair rides when they were kids. Squeezing her eyes closed again, she lifted her hand to bat at the alarm clock on the nightstand.

What the hell was the noise?

Where the hell was the clock? The nightstand?

She opened her eyes again. The room was dark, only a crack of daylight showed through the closed drapes.

"What the hell?" she mumbled as she pushed herself up on her elbows. She peeled her tongue off the roof of her mouth and tried to swallow. But she was drier than the fried chicken her grandma used to serve on the nights she babysat Sheridan and the boys.

The sheet slid low enough to feel cool air. On her skin. On her breasts.

Shit.

She was naked.

And her alarm clock and her nightstand were not where they were supposed to be.

She flinched when someone moved beside her in the bed.

"What time is it?" the male voice grumbled.

Whatdididowhatdididowhatdidido?

"No idea," she mumbled. The noise—that jack hammering that woke her up—had faded some, but she could still hear it. *Feel* it. In the base of her skull. Not a jack hammer. She had a headache, one *hell of a headache.*

The person beside her in bed moved a bit, and suddenly golden lamplight lit the room.

Her stomach roiled.

Not just a headache.

Sheridan gagged as she moved closer to the edge of the bed and slipped her leg out from under the sheets. She pressed her toes to the floor, but the room kept spinning. Skimming a hand down her belly, between her legs confirmed it.

Still naked.

Complete, birthday suit, nudity.

"Shit." The male groaned beside her. "What the hell were we drinking?"

Sheridan squeezed her eyes closed again. The last thing she remembered was an Irish Car Bomb. And AC/DC blaring.

Somebody was shooting pool. A motorcycle guy. He'd had a red bandana. Big beard.

Her stomach turned again.

Had she been so drunk she'd come home with him? Had she actually climbed onto a motorcycle with a drunk guy? Jesus, thirty-five years old, and she still squirmed at the thought of what her mother would have to say about that.

"Tequila shots," the guy beside her groaned.

"No," she argued. "Irish Car Bombs."

"Mm-hmm." He hummed his agreement. "And then tequila shots."

"Why?" She flopped back on her pillow and rubbed her hands over her eyes. Why had she thought that was a good idea? For fuck's sake, she wasn't a kid. She knew when to stop drinking. She could hold her liquor. She knew better than to mix liquor like that, and she hadn't gone home with a random guy in a good eight years, if not longer.

The thought of that raggedy beard dragging over her skin made her shudder. She knew a lot of women were into that hillbilly beard look. As far as she was concerned, those women could have them all. She wasn't attracted to that sort of man or beard.

"Dunno."

"Just tell me we didn't—"

"We did." He interrupted her. "I do remember that."

She snorted.

"Yeah, I got that."

He laughed softly, clearly amused by her.

"Did we ride your motorcycle here?"

"I don't have a motorcycle," he answered, "And no. Neither of us drove. Some guy dumped us off here."

That made her nerves flutter a bit. No motorcycle? The guy she was remembering was definitely in a gang. He had the leather jacket, some kind of lettering on it. Sheridan couldn't remember now what it said, but she remembered tracing the stitching with her fingers.

Who the hell was in bed beside her? And who the hell had brought them here?

"Who?" She tried again to swallow, but her mouth was still dry as cotton.

"Mav."

"Oh." She breathed a bit deeper, a *little* bit of relief loosening her shoulders. Maverick Pressey was from the area. He lived in Rodey, not far from Kissing Springs. She knew him, though not well, since he was younger, probably closer to her brother Rhett's age. She didn't remember seeing him at the Iron Stag last night, but he did frequent the place, so it was probable.

"Okay." She sighed and tried again to sit up. "Well. I need to get outta here."

"Don't run away on my account."

She snorted and ran her hands through her hair. "Trust me. I'm half drunk and half hungover, and I don't think you want that mess in your bed."

"That may be true," he spoke softly, absently, like he was tired. She jumped when she felt his fingers brush her lower back. "But I don't mind you in my bed."

"Nice try." She tucked her hair behind her ears and looked at the floor. An area rug covered old hardwood. Neat enough on this side of the bed, but Sheridan was ready to get the hell out of here. Slip on her clothes and do the walk of shame and put this disaster behind her.

She eased off the bed cautiously, aware of Irish Car Bombs and shots of tequila and God only knew what else was sloshing around in her body while she had no idea where the bathroom was.

"What're you doing?"

"Looking for my clothes."

"Mmm."

She glanced at him over her shoulder. Still lying down, face nearly buried in his pillow, she could only make out dark hair. A touch of scruff on his face, but not a full beard. Another wave of relief, followed by anger at herself.

Really, Sheridan? You have no idea who you slept with last night, but you're gonna be thankful it wasn't the guy with the beard?

"Any ideas?" she asked him.

"No. I barely remembered stumbling inside."

"But you remember having sex with me?" She tipped her head and rolled her eyes.

"Not like I'm gonna forget how loud you screamed my name. Four times, to be exact."

She knew his name?

"Shit." She sighed and turned her attention back to finding her clothes. When she still didn't see anything on the floor closer to the door, she flipped the overhead light on.

"Aww. Man." He groaned. "Give a guy a warning, Sheridan."

He knew her name.

Fuck.

"Mmm." She noticed a scrap of lace just outside the bedroom door. "Hard to find black underwear in the dark."

She snatched her panties up and stepped into them.

"I think your bra might be in the kitchen."

"The kitchen?"

"No. Maybe on the lamp in the living room." His voice was familiar, but it wasn't someone she knew well. Not someone she had grown up with here.

"Seriously?"

"It was pretty incredible, and frankly, Sheridan, I'm a bit offended that you don't remember."

She barked a laugh and turned again just as he shoved the comforter and sheet off and climbed out of bed. Gloriously naked, he stretched his arms over his head. It was kind of a shame she didn't remember what they had done. Even now, she could imagine what kind of lover he was.

She dragged her eyes up over his body and met his gaze.

"Fuck."

Want to read the rest of Sheridan & Trey's story? Click here.

also by tracy broemmer

Women's Fiction Novels:

Luther's Cross 10th Anniversary Edition

Just Like Them

Small Hours

Picket Fences

Two Story Home

Say Everything

Sketching Litchfield Lake

Damsel

The Valentine Suite

Fairytale

Green-Eyed Girl

Come Home For Christmas

Ever, Again

Safe as Houses

Every Little Thing, Lorelei Bluffs, Book 1

Two A.M., Lorelei Bluffs, Book 2

Blind, Lorelei Bluffs, Book 3

Leaving July, Lorelei Bluffs, Book 4

Hesitation Marks, Lorelei Bluffs, Book 5

Four Letter Words, Lorelei Bluffs, Book 6

See Kate, Lorelei Bluffs, Book 7

Loved You More, Lorelei Bluffs, Book 8

A Lorelei Ending, Lorelei Bluffs, Book 9

I Do, Lorelei Bluffs, Book 10

Truth Is, The Williams Legacy, Book 1

Other People's Ugly, The Williams Legacy, Book 2

Omissions, The Williams Legacy, Book 3

Contemporary Romance Novels:

Destiny's Calling: Your Future Is Waiting

Wedding Day Shenanigans

Holiday Fling

The Kiss Off

Something Like Love

Plus One

Hold Onto the Stars, Book #5 in Blue Collar Romance series

The Jane Thing, Book #2 in Meet Cute Book Club series

Doctor Divine, Doctors of Eastport General, Season 2

Beach Daze, Flamingo Island

Moonlight in Montreal, The Vagabond Series

Christmas and Other Inconveniences, Betting on Christmas Collection

A Naughty Lesson, Most Eligible Bachelors

Eggnog in Amesbury, Christmas in Amesbury Series (SWEET ROMANCE)

A December Wish, Wishing for Love Series (SWEET ROMANCE)

Shameless Santa, Kissing Springs Bourbon Fever Collection, Book 1

Sunshine & Soulmates, Kissing Springs Bourbon Fever Collection, Book 2

Bourbon & Bedposts, Kissing Springs Bourbon Fever Collection, Book 3

Midnight AND Mercy, Kissing Springs Bourbon Fever Collection, Book 4

Love, Nashville, The Mississippi Queen Trilogy, Book 1

Forever, Duncan, The Mississippi Queen Trilogy, Book 2

Always, Jess, The Mississippi Queen Trilogy, Book 3

Gettin' Hitched, The H Books, Book 1

Hookin' Up, The H Books, Book 2

Holdin' On, The H Books, Book 2.5

Intoxicate Me, 515 Whiskey, Book .5

Taste Me, 515 Whiskey, Book 1

Contemporary Romance Novellas:

Indian Summer

Dear Jaclyn Perris

French Stuff

End in Flames

Mistletoe Mishaps

Toasted: A New Year's Eve Novella

Boone's Girl

Trusting Cupid

Makin' Whoopsie!

Swipe for Fangs

Swipe for Ghouls

Feels on Wheels (Love in Motion Duet, Book 1)(SWEET ROMANCE)

Rings on Wings (Love in Motion Duet, Book 2) (SWEET ROMANCE)

Love in Motion Duet Boxset (SWEET ROMANCE)

Endless Summer (Timberton Hounds)

Homeless Holiday (Timberton Hounds)

Restless Hearts (Timberton Hounds)

The Timberton Hounds Novellas Boxset

Seducing You (Welcome to Kissing Springs: Bourbon Fever & Lockland Distilling: Keys to Love Trilogy)

Kissing You (Welcome to Kissing Springs: Bourbon Fever & Lockland Keys to Love Trilogy)

Other Novellas:

The Devy Man, A Horror Novella

Today, Again (Sweet Love Story)

Women's Fiction Short Stories:

India Falls

Luther's Cross: 87,600

The Candy Cane Tree of Willow Lane

Delays

Same Time Next Year

Contemporary Romance Short Stories:

Perfect Pictures, The Wine Tasting Series, Traminette (SWEET)

Coming Home, The Wine Tasting Series, Edelweiss (SWEET)

Save Me Every Dance, The Wine Tasting Series, Rosé (SWEET)

Marry Me, The Wine Tasting Series, Shiraz (SWEET)

Birthday Wishes, The Wine Tasting Series, Muscat (SWEET)

Dad Jeans, The Wine Tasting Series, Vignoles (SWEET))

The Wine Tasting Series Boxset (SWEET)

Peppermint Lane

Priceless Memory (Timberton Hounds)

Truly Dante, A Mississippi Queen Trilogy short story

Strawberry Wine

Love Letter

Leaving You, Welcome to Kissing Springs: Bourbon Fever & Lockland Distilling: Keys to Love short story

Sambuca Santa

Deadman's Hollow

about the author

Tracy is the author of several contemporary romance titles, including Plus One, Wedding Day Shenanigans, The Mississippi Queen Trilogy, and the H Books—Gettin' Hitched, Hookin' Up, and Holdin' On. Tracy also writes women's fiction and is the author of the Williams Legacy series as well as several stand-alone titles.

Tracy's books have been called gripping, emotional, and timely, and readers describe her characters as real and relatable.

Tracy lives in Midwestern Illinois with her husband of 31 years.

Find her on the web at www.broemmerbooks.com

www.ingramcontent.com/pod-product-compliance
Lightning Source LLC
LaVergne TN
LVHW091135080826
845145LV00008B/2160